Victims

a novel by Travis Jeppesen

Akashic Books
New York

Fic

Published by Akashic Books
©2003 Travis Jeppesen

ISBN: 1-888451-42-4
Library of Congress Control Number: 2002116776
Cover photograph by Joel Westendorf
All rights reserved
First printing
Printed in Canada

Little House on the Bowery
c/o Akashic Books
PO Box 1456
New York, NY 10009
Akashic7@aol.com
www.akashicbooks.com

Acknowledgments

I'm grateful to Dennis Cooper for believing when no one else cared; to everyone from the Berlin days, especially Bertie Marshall, Peter Shevlin, Sue de Beer, Nick Mauss, Kenneth Okiishi, Keith Spedding, John Haas, and Michael Martarano; to Bruce Benderson, Elizabeth Blackburn, Deborah Jeppesen, Jon Jeppesen, Joshua Cohen, and the numerous shadows from my adolescence.

Special thanks to Philip Guichard for sharing the ride.

X

Y

He who loves his life will lose it, and he who hates his life in this world will keep it for eternal life.

—John 12:25

ADOLESCENCE

(TANYA & HERBERT)

The telephone rings. There's nothing else to do, so I answer it. *Yeah?* It's L.D. He wants me to come over, but I don't know. All we ever do is watch TV and fuck. I can watch TV at home and get myself off better than any guy. Two weeks ago, he tried to fuck me without a condom. That's all I need, to be pregnant with his kid. My parents. They'd force me to have it. It's bad enough as it is, having Jesus shoved down my throat on a daily basis. Makes me wanna barf. I don't even like sex that much, I just love him and wanna make him happy, even though he bores me most of the time. He's still better than the majority of what I'm surrounded by. I tell him I can't come over and hang up. We'll see each other at school tomorrow anyway.

Eight o'clock in the morning, science class, teacher is a fat old black bitch with purple hairs sticking out the top of her head. She's totally senile and always fucks up everyone's name. She calls me Delila for some reason and L.D. L.P. We just giggle and ignore her. She is a total bitch, though. My mom told me that they've been trying to fire her for years, but they can't cos she's black and has tenure.

Anyway, L.D. has some glue, so I throw out my turkey sandwich and we squirt some in the bag and duck down under the lab table. Pretty soon, we're seeing dots floating around us and it's like our brains have been lifted to another dimension and Mrs. Roseboro keeps going on and on about the elements on the periodic table and me and L.D. can't look at each other without laughing.

Herbert falls into holes quite often. When you're down in the ditch, dwelling in your own sacrilege isn't gonna get you out of it. In the end it is always best to fall down. Nonetheless, he finds himself drenched in memory, past lives colliding with his inability to live in the moment.

The Purple Goat Ceremony only occurred once every astral generation. Herbert had started the day by picking flowers in the field behind the compound, the only outdoor location deemed acceptable by the classroom. The field lay across a few acres. A bunch of weeds living in houses made of dead grass. Intended for recreation, it provided a beautiful alternative to the web of sterile hallways aligning the interior of the compound, though it remained empty throughout the year, even when spring commenced exhaling her warm breath into the cold, desolate climate.

The compound was housed in the building of the former Buick Elementary School, which had closed its doors when the town dried up following the economic recession of the early '90s. It was as though a dark cloud had settled over this town, or the cosmos were conspiring to deface its fate. It started with an industrial labor strike at the Buick Mercury factory which was never properly arbitrated. Then, rather suddenly, there was an accident in the school that set the tone for the town's demise.

Some fireworks exploded in a locker. One student, whose name was Bliff, had been unlucky enough to be standing next to the locker at the time of the explosion. Some metal flew into his eyes, culminating in blindness. Many of the other students had been traumatized by the sight of blood squirting out of his eye sockets, also by the pitch of Bliff's screams—for having known Bliff quite well, they had never heard him scream. Following a suite of drawn-out, ultimately unsuccessful lawsuits filed by a handful of financially desperate parents, the school was closed shortly thereafter. The Buick citizens found themselves with no jobs and no school to send their young'uns to, and migrated elsewhere in search of something. Anything.

When the Overcomers moved in, paying rent via an inheritance that one of the group's members had donated, they removed all of the equipment from what used to be the playground, leaving a completely barren field, still and ugly. Most of them appeared to be intimidated by its openness, preferring the serene privacy of their living quarters to such a direct confrontation with the sun. Herbert was the only one who would occasionally go out there to sun himself, stare up at the pale gray sky, pensive, blank.

Herbert brought the flowers in to his mother. She was seated on the cheap knitted couch at the rear of the room, her hands fitted together in a tight clasp. Dwelling quarters consisted of a single cell for each familial unit. Luckily for Herbert and his mother, it was just the two of them. The tight accommodations had taught the two something about survival, but what that something is, no one is really sure. Their Teacher had deemed it necessary to minimize the sleeping compartments—each was given just a small enclave—because the joiners kept joining, popping out babies left and right, who were in turn having babies of their own, and nobody ever left.

School comes to an end, and the bus drops us off back where we started. Suburban inferno. No escape, no exit doors. We put off going home for as long as we can, cos there's absolutely nothing to do there, TV and telephone, maybe, that's all. So we take a long walk and talk and smoke lots of cigarettes, maybe walk through the woods, down to the creek and make out. L.D. always wants to go further than I want to go. I don't understand what's with guys, why they have to go there every time. It's like total madness. I mean, I never get that horny, no girls I know of have even had sex yet. I know he loves me, so I don't really mind, I just don't want to do it every goddamn day.

What else is there to do? Until we're old enough to drive, we're basically trapped here. L.D.'s parents are never around, and my parents won't drive me to anything that's not church-related.

They're always building new houses in our neighborhood, and it usually takes them a really long time. It's a complicated process since the whole neighborhood is surrounded by a forest, so they have to knock down the trees and clear the lot first before they even start building, then the actual construction can take like six or seven months.

So when we're really bored and desperate, we go play in

the houses at night, after the construction workers are long gone. We mainly just do stupid stuff, like throw bricks at each other, tear down the plaster off the walls, draw shit on the floors with leftover paint.

Sometimes I wonder what all this'll look like a thousand years from now. All these houses look the same, two-story brick monsters, with only slightly different characteristics. The garage might be in back of a house instead of on the side, or the shutters are painted a different shade of blue. I guess there will be more and more houses until the forest is all gone and there's no more creek for the kids to play in, no more skeletal foundations of houses to destroy, just coming home after school every day to stare at the wall and wonder what Mom's cooking for dinner.

A flash of light bends over the scene. Herbert's foot falls on a daisy. It is all, in a breathy word, senseless: the day, the flower, the cows in the field, memories of past perceptions and present awareness of self melting into each other like two different characters who are really the same person . . . How perplexing time may seem when you're standing on its face. In retaliation to the boredom that enslaves him, Herbert begins to burn flowers in the field he is standing in, the new field that has replaced the old one of his childhood. The cows look up when they smell the roasting funk. It hits their big wide sinuses like the taste of a lit match.

Victims

I'm standing in front of my mirror naked staring at myself. I smeared black eyeliner around my eyes cos I thought it'd make me look sexy, but it doesn't work, I just look like some cheap whore. I'm sure L.D. would love it. I gave him head for the first time the other day and now he's on this blowjob kick, wants me to do it all the time. I'd rather he just fuck me cos it's a lot less work. He never really eats me out, and when he does, it only lasts for like a minute before he has to get his thing out.

Anyway, I'm studying my body in the mirror. I wish my tits were bigger. I'm such a freak. I don't know why I decided to dye my hair black. At the time, it seemed like a good idea, but now my skin is way too pale. I look blue. Totally sickly, like I'm dying or some shit. Maybe it doesn't matter. I wish I could transform myself into someone else, just disappear into another body for a while. I'm getting fatter, too. There's no way in hell my hips were that wide last month. My stomach used to be flat and smooth, but now there's a roll of flab there. So fucking disgusting.

Okay, so the other thing is I haven't gotten my period in two weeks. I think it's just cos my body's fucked up, I haven't been sleeping or eating much lately, taking lots of caffeine tablets. If I don't get it by tomorrow, I go into panic mode.

Herbert walked the length of the field. Forest in front of him, he stepped off the edge and continued walking. Herbert knew this was forbidden. The penalties were harsh. He didn't care for some reason. He had studied authority his whole life. Understood the fact that authority is only there when it wants something from you. There was nothing that could be asked of Herbert. No authorities ever came searching for him. It was like he didn't exist, as though he were merely a shell in a pile of shells. Maybe that's how he'd felt his whole life.

Anyway, how else could the task be accomplished? The Goat wouldn't be found in the field. Thus, Herbert had to leave the property. His mother knew how risky this was considered; if anyone from the outside world was made aware of where they lived, it could put their task in great peril. It was a risk, but it wasn't her risk, so in a sense it didn't matter.

Who knew if she and Herbert would even have the same relationship in the Next Level? There was no evidence to suggest they would. In the Bible, Jesus addressed his most important messages to individuals, not groups. She realized how important he was, as her son, from a cellular perspective, while respecting the fact that she would never truly be able to identify with him. Relationships of any sort were looked upon as symptoms—or more specifically, desperate failures—of the human world—something they were trying to get past.

Anyway, Herbert was happy to traipse new fertility. Months afterward, he'd take his second jaunt off the property. From there, he'd never return.

Oh, modern life is so mundane. Although that may be a per-verted, snobbish thing to think, Herbert doesn't care. He has separated himself from everything: spirit from visage, past from present—a healthy dosage of ammunition. Mother fig-ure a stunning beauty. Sometimes he misses her, despite himself. She had taught him something about memory, a thing that would not be forgotten. The something in her eyes. Humanity, Love, Affection: She had felt them all, and maybe she had even felt something else. Who knows what she felt like on the inside. Herbert only recalls what she felt like on the outside.

To call her Mother is not totally correct. Although the bio-logical bond couldn't be denied, and wasn't, the mainte-nance of traditional familial relationships was discouraged. It was viewed as another obstruction to the final goal, neces-sary to "get beyond," and they did it without questioning. They were more like molecules belonging to a larger cellular unit. This is how they had learned to view themselves.

Then there was the night of Micky Tim's birthday. Micky was the biological son of Turnip, the music officer. Turnip was the only black member of the Overcomers. Except for the color of his skin, his outer appearance conformed to ev-eryone else's (shaved head, white robe), other than the indiscreet presence of a golden earring dangling from his left earlobe. As a student, many years before finding the Overcomers, he had been involved with the Black Power movement. He joined a Back to Africa crusade at his university, his comrades encouraging his thesis on American slavery. One of the things that baffled him the most was the fact that, at the end of the Civil War, many former slaves, having been granted their freedom, chose to stay put and continue working for their masters. Supposedly, they did this out of love and devotion to their former owners, but also out of fear of life outside of servitude, the life they had been born and bred into. The world outside was still cold and hostile, leaving subservience as the only feasible option. As a symbol of their compliance, they would wear a golden ring in their left ear.

Having himself experienced this cruel world the freed slaves were so reluctant to join, Turnip found his lost master in Martin Jones, Earth's Representative from the Next Level of Existence. The significance of his obtuse golden appendage was thus known and accepted by all.

The Elder Council came up with the brilliant idea of organizing a karaoke birthday party for Micky, using songs about the spacecraft that Turnip had written. And Turnip tickled those ivories unlike he ever had before. Tina Jones accidentally ate a fingernail and barfed. She had to go to bed, missing out on a chance to sing "Jesus Wants Me for a Moonbeam." (By what measure will the moonbeam rise?!) And so the party went on. And on and on and on and on and on. And on and on and on and on and on and on and on. And on.

Hours later, mother and son lay side-by-side in bed, drained from their involvement in the celebration. Half-asleep, hand accidentally fell on her son's inner thigh. A white light entering through the window lightly brushed the sterile interior of the room, flushed in a harness of darkness chokingly tightened by the strain underlying the . . . scenario. Inside the compound, thirty-seven sleeping bodies, each with a black burn on the left shoulder. A harmonic medley, fat and thin, of breaths oozing out of mouths in unison, like pus from an infected wound. The lights from the moonbeam touching. But only Herbert awake to see.

Today I looked in the mirror and said to myself, *You know what, Tanya? You look like shit. You're always going to look like shit, and nothing you can do will ever change that. So why care so much? Why even bother? It doesn't mean you're a bad person. You have a great boyfriend who loves you, something that none of your friends have, so what does it matter if you're never going to win any beauty contests?*

And then my mother bursts through the door (without knocking, of course), grabs me by the hair, and slaps me really hard, so hard that I fall on the floor. Fucking hysterical, as usual, screaming and crying, telling me I'm going to hell.

Dad had opened the refrigerator in the garage, where he keeps his extra beer, and discovered it missing. It didn't take them long to put two and two together, it never does. I don't know why I'm so stupid.

So I'm not allowed to go out this weekend, and I have to go to church and Sunday school. I fucking hate my mom, the fat bitch, and I know she hates me, too. My dad, I don't know, he just sits on the couch and drinks beer all night when he gets home from work. At least he's not all uptight like Mom is.

My worst fear is that I'll grow up to become fat like her. She's such a disgusting person. I know it's wrong, but sometimes I just wish she'd hurry up and die. It'd make my life a hell of a lot easier.

Something moving behind that tree. Herbert held the burlap sack in his sweaty hands, which trembled with fear. From behind the trunk, two shiny black horns emerged, followed by the Goat's ashy gray face. *Those horns could kill me,* Herbert thought to himself. The Goat froze, staring at Herbert. Herbert was trying to make the voices in his head go away. *When you go to the fields, be sure to reap the rewards of your brethren. Service to Your Father equals victory in the highest possible sense of the word.* Herbert had been told that the Goat was a sacred messenger sent to Earth by their astral leaders, the high commanders of the Next Level. It would be honored tonight in a ceremony, its message transmitted through their bodies upon consumption. Perhaps now was the time they had all been waiting for, the Goat's flesh the disguise of the spacecraft that would take them away, to live in forever, that suspended moment of perpetual victory.

Herbert stepped toward the Goat. It immediately turned and began petering off in the opposite direction, revealing its burgundy fleece while forcing Herbert to assume a similar pace, galloping toward the swift quadruped with the hole of his sack extended. Suddenly, he tripped over a stone and fell face first. But not even this blow would knock some sense into Young Herbert: He stood up and kept going with unflinching determination. He'd chase it into the ocean if that's what it took to catch the skuzzy itling. The ceremony could not begin without its presence. Herbert refused to think of the consequences.

The Goat slowed down and began to drool. Its beard became wet with a sticky substance as Herbert nearly had a heart attack.

Poor Herbert finally caught up with the ugly thing and was within grasping distance when a loud *bah!* was emitted from its mouth, all but startling the young boy into oblivion; nonetheless, he was eventually able to grab it, envelope its head in the sack, whereupon he removed from his left pocket a syringe filled with Ketamine and proceeded to stab the thing in the neck. The Goat went limp in his arms. He dragged it off toward home.

Herbert slammed the door shut behind him and shook some sweat off his forehead, fatigued. After all, having to drag a small monstrosity across the length of a field is quite depriving, quite depriving indeed! Herbert dropped the furry carcass on the rug in the center of the room and fell into bed, hoping sleep would heal his aches and worries, but it didn't. He was too hungry to sleep.

He tore the blankets off of himself angrily, spitting on the bed he shared with his mother. Irrational fits of anger often took hold of his entire being, during the course of which unorthodox catharses would arise, inexplicable even to Herbert himself, only to be tempered with age, when blind acceptance and complacency melts over the hatred we once felt so strongly under the strain of youth.

He walked into the kitchen and removed a butcher knife from the drawer. Flipping the Goat over on its back, Herbert remarked how pale its skin was beneath the violet fur as he sank the blade in and proceeded to rip its stomach open. The Goat choked and kicked him in the forehead. Herbert fell back, but not for long, for as soon as his ass kissed the ground, he immediately bounced back up to stab the Goat four or five more times before collapsing on top of it, the fire inside him finally extinguished.

Scratching his head, he focused on the blood on his fingers in order to think. He came to the conclusion that, while all this had been quite fulfilling, he was still hungry.

He reached into the Goat's stomach and pulled out a warm glob of kidney, which he bit into and chewed on for a second or two. Its consistency was identical to that of bacon, and was therefore easy to swallow and digest. He didn't even mind the intimate taste. In fact, he revered its originality— he had never before tasted such an exotic delicacy.

As he drifted off to sleepland, he saw androids floating past him in his dreams. He had suddenly been transported to another realm, and in it he deciphered shadows of distant figures he knew—there's Tanya and Martin and Turnip and the others—only they were no longer in human form, but mutated into grotesque objects half lifeless and half mammalistic. They were donning identical hoods just as they had in waking life, but now the hoods were brown, instead of white. This minor feature would later remind Herbert of a recent episode of that TV show, the one they were allowed to watch, the government's conspiracy to suppress other life forms under the false guise of protection of the species . . .

When he awoke, his mother's face hovered over him, her wide brown eyes gazing down.

Where is it? she queried her young son, whose breath smelled suspiciously like a motel air conditioner.

In my stomach, he replied, unable to tell a lie.

The chandelier turned on in a too-bright fashion, temporarily blinding his blurred half-asleep eyes into a painful focus. At that moment, he regretted all the moments that had come before. Herbert wanted to keep a distanced view of things, yet at times, coherence could not be reached. Nothing in the past applied to the present moment.

She ran out back, hoping that her son was playing a devilish prank on her.

He wasn't. Herbert had indeed eaten the majority of the sacred Goat. Its guts she found out back rotting beneath the solar inferno, like a castrated bull's offerings to the sun god (or the hot grill of a tapas bar). He had put the entire classroom in spiritual jeopardy.

They kept him locked up in a janitorial closet, no food, only a glass of water twice a day, for the duration of one week. When it became evident that nothing was happening, no message being transmitted, they began to speak to him, asking him questions about the taste of the Goat, where he had found it, what it had looked like when he found it, what he thought led him to it, until the questions assumed a cryptically threatening tone. He was also castigated for leaving the property, which was of course considered a betrayal.

Then, on Saturday at midnight, Martin unlocked the closet door and silently led him down the hallway to his room. Mysteriously, his mother was absent. He sat on the bed, totally exhausted, patiently waiting for her return.

When he woke up the next morning, he was still alone. This was all highly unusual, to say the least, he had no idea where he was supposed to be or if he was even supposed to be and so he immediately put his clothes on and went out into the hallway to find it empty, calm. He decided to wander around a bit, but he couldn't find anyone and he was scared, so he went back into the room, sat down, and stared out the window, occasionally chewing on his thumbnail, until she finally returned, greeting him with a silent hostility.

In the weeks that followed, Herbert was treated with an aphonic distance. That is to say, he was ignored by all, including his own mother, although life went on normally in every other respect.

For the first time in his life, Herbert was able to form one or two ideas of his own, and found that he didn't mind one bit.

L.D. has this stupid idea that we're in a band. He plays guitar and I'm supposed to sing. I can't sing worth shit so I end up just screaming half the time like my fucking teeth are on fire and he thinks it's great, so whatev.

All our songs so far are really short, like two minutes long. We have this one song called "Jenny" about this girl who moves to a new town and doesn't have any friends so she jumps off a bridge. We have another song called "Travis's Rash" about this guy at our school who has this gnarly rash on his face. Then there's "Let's Start a Forest Fire." Our other songs are sped-up Christmas carols.

So the other night after "band practice" (kind of a silly notion, considering the fact that we're not really a band cos it's just the two of us), we were sitting on the couch in his basement, watching TV, smoking. He had shorts on but no underwear underneath, so I looked over and his thing was hanging out, and it just pissed me off for some reason. Then he started rubbing it and touching my leg, and I knew what was coming next, so I just told him. I'm preg.

He looked at me like I'm crazy. *No you're not.*

I haven't gotten my period in two months.

He stood up and started pacing around. Then he sat down in a chair on the other side of the room. *I think you should go. I* didn't know what to say, so I got up and left, went home, fell asleep.

The flowers flame with a soaring intensity. Some of the cows begin to drift away from the smoke. It eventually follows them, according to the shifting state of the wind, because it is faster than them.

Beneath Herbert's feet are holes. Tiny tiny holes. Although he is unable to feel them, he imagines he can. Until he exaggerates their size in his head to the extent that he finds himself falling into a soil puncture from where a weed once emerged before a hungry calf bent over and snatched it away.

A few smoky clouds hang over the horizon. The sky is crystal pale. Holes everywhere. The sky. All mothers, even the Virgin.

What would he do when his body had filled one of these holes, tumbling down, nearly breaking his neck on one or two occasion(s)? To ask Herbert this question is to slap his face with a blank. The only cog of the whole routine that holds much significance to him is the in-motion-falling part. The messy joy of a trip. The sideline adrenaline rush of an athletic binge . . . Down. He thinks about the shapes and sizes of different holes he could fall down into, holes that contain entrances to corridors of different worlds. He picks a weed and bites it with his hind teeth, trying to avoid its eventual brush 'gainst the tongue.

His mother always slept in a curved position, on her side, which made her appear elegant, of course, from an aerial perspective, her body a ghost, a thrift shape moving beneath a white sheet. Whenever he fucked her, he'd enter softly yet stubbornly, with the awkwardness of a young child's blurred vision. She'd release a soft sigh, and then he'd discharge inside her, his dick so close to the womb he had once been small enough to fit inside of. When cumming, Herbert always felt as though he had never seen white. Although he really had no idea what was happening (thought he was dying or something), intimations of eternal sin flushed him with a sense of guilt, flashing on and off like a neon sign in the dark. The devil's reward, sensation, is a cruel tempter. The chocolate of the spirit. Contradictory impulses flooded the scene. A part of him needed to shoot and shoot again: already damned. A consideration of sudden material freedom, drifting through life a negative specimen. An emergence from safety. Here and there, words float restlessly, too fast and thorough to capture individually . . . Shadows of bodies in dark corners . . . Naked. He recognized that he secretly wanted to get lost in every crevice he could manage to come across . . . Track down the damp darkness . . . Hide on the inside of another's body . . . or just an insertion in the landscape.

That was how Herbert came to choose the predetermined Second Life. He told his mother goodbye in a memorably secret way: He announced his intention to go walking in the field "for a little while" on that arbitrarily chosen day. His pace quickened as he trailed further and further away from the compound, and tears formed in the corners of his eyes. Memories infiltrated his thoughts as he ran through the forest: Mama's bald head, her vagina; the Goat he had eaten, his remarkable failure to preserve even the heart for the ceremonial proceedings; the unmentionable deed; a white line shot across the sky, following an airplane's descent; oh, all his major failures.

He hasn't looked back since. Or made any attempt to contact her. To this day, she is still the only woman who has ever had much of a lasting presence in his life.

As hunger starts to attack, Herbert leaves the field, walks home, cooks some fish. He caught it in the lake in the next town over, which provides the undemanding Monkhole water supply . . . A whore drowned there long ago, Howard once told him . . . He drops the silver-scaled monstrosities down along the slab of grill in his backyard, under which charcoal burns, emitting thick black smoke and a gaseous scent, slightly resembling the odor of burning shit, and as the perfume makes its prominent entrance into the smellosphere, one can taste this fish by merely breathing, such is its nascent effect on the sinuses.

In the evening, Herbert has a lot of time on his hands. He chooses to spend these hours working on small projects around the house. He also likes to cook a sound meal and consume it all by himself. Sometimes, he stands in his backyard and looks up at the stars. Other times, he will drink beer till he snottily pukes. Occasionally, his friend Ruphis will venture out to Herbert's home and the two will sit silently reminiscing while the sun goes down and the mosquitoes begin to gobble them up. When he's standing or sitting outside, he chews on blades of grass because he likes the way it tastes, even though he knows the soil is made out of dead animals decomposing from the years of evolution. Nature is a fine thing. So is the whore! Waterfalls go down on people's heads. Frogs croak at night near the swamps. A porch light stays on, and another, and a third . . .

An entire country with back porch-lights on in the middle of the night.

It doesn't pay to think about certain things. Memories: You have to care about something, even if you're trying to destroy it. Crack open another beer, enjoy self immensely, grim look on the face to spite it all . . .

Sometimes he wonders if she's still alive. Or if they killed her. Or if they evolved. Anything's possible.

Herbert picks up a fork, stabs the burnt fish, removes it quickly from the grill, and sets it on the plate, all the while trying to forget. Smoke grows toward his face. He pushes the brown grill-cover down to smother the smoke, raises a knife in his left hand, sinking its blade into the charred fish's fin. It inserts nicely, and as the knifepoint stabs some fried internal organ, a tiny bubble pops out of the fish's gaping mouth. Its eyeball, too, still intact. Staring absently at the stars. A rather clear night. Remarkable enough for Herbert to notice. Herbert wonders if the fish can see it, even as he bites into it. Oh, how delicious that fish is! It gives him such a delightful thrill, knowing he caught it himself—a simple economic exchange, the fish's death for Herbert's life. He spits out a bone and burps.

Thus, Herbert's life is a progression through oblatory phases. He had begun communally interned to the lords floating above him, ran away from that lord farm to spend the rest of his life asking questions. Life became its own sort of monastery. Now Herbert worships cows. He grabs his balls and looks to the sky. True romance up there. The Mother in a beautiful form. He would get into the skies one day, even if it killed him trying. His whole life, he yearned for goodness. God sends a secular message: *Eat cheap fish*. God says some very odd things.

Why is it that I fucked my mother? I wasn't there, it was another body in another place. Displacement of geographical conditions. Going nowhere, you can be in every place at once. Swallow God. Halo harkens. God has controlled every root of my hallucination.

Trapped within the guise of "old" age, Herbert recently discovered masturbation. Cold cream is a necessary commodity, purchased on the few occasions he ventures out to the store, the only store in Monkhole, similar to the convenience mart in Buick. Destinations are weak. The same wind flows through each one. Monkhole or Chicago, it doesn't matter. A place is a place. The same people, the same faiths.

Herbert is glad to be where he is, even though it seems at times to be the middle of nowhere. A free mind, free sensibility. Always open to the more precarious forms of knowledge, a hopeless intellect, a house and a tree. Lawless nightmare: the same cries, the same prayers, the same hopeless people.

I don't know what to do now. I think I'm going crazy, to be honest, totally losing it.

L.D. hasn't called me in weeks and has been ignoring me, which isn't too difficult cos he just got a car and has been driving it to school every day. And he's never home. Who knows where he's going.

I've never felt so alone. And I can feel the kid inside me, I'm getting fatter and I get sick in the mornings and have to be quiet about it so my parents won't hear. But it's only a matter of weeks before it becomes really obvious, they're gonna figure it out.

I'm in such deep shit.

Truth be told, Herbert no longer knows who he is and no longer cares.

He takes another beer out of the refrigerator.

Eating raw goat had made young Herbert quite sick, quite sick indeed. His malady was deep enough to terminate any desire for carnivorous consumption in the years to come. Fish are okay: a fish is not a meat. But a cow is, as is raw goat. Animals are there to be stared at, not eaten.

Herbert's political views are limited by infinity. Indeed, there is not much to consider in Monkhole, as the organization of such practical alliances had been deemed needless (that is to say, if this idea had been deemed anything, or even thought of before). Herbert's thoughts tend to border on the abstract. That is to say . . . if he has any thoughts at all. Some would say Milkweed has more thoughts.

Herbert's penis is small, crooked, and shaped like a hook in an odd way. When he rubs it, it shoots white worms out with the speed and ferocity of a bullet. These white worms, he knows from a pseudo–sex education course given to the children of the Overcomers every year, have lives in them. And to offer a life to a woman is not always a good thing. Once inside, the white worm opens up, infecting the body with a second life, like a kangaroo. The woman hops around screaming till a child breaks through her bleeding egg, screaming its fucking head off.

He has shot white worms into a few whores, yet that had been nothing much to speak of. Just getting his rocks off for the umpteenth time, a seweral haven for the ladders in hell. He loves to fuck something that feels good while she blinks an eye. Voice is important, too. If a whore has a pretty sound, he is in heaven.

Sometimes Herbert metamorphoses into a cow, eating the filthy autumn leaves scattered along the field and mooing into the dusk. Another caretaker then stands above him, keeping watch just as Herbert keeps watch when he is not a cow.

Herbert remembers the last week he spent with his mother. The lingering odor of disinfectant, tinged with the presence of a silent angst, it had all begun to sicken him. Then there were the final days, when the silence was broken with a tense chaos that erupted as unexpectedly as a geyser. Of course, communication was limited to violent gesture, so as not to disturb the calm of daily life in the compound. Talking was prohibited except for when it was absolutely necessary to say something. Their Father had informed them that oral communication was unnecessary in the Next Level, and their lives on Earth were to be spent in preparation for becoming what they were destined to become.

It became increasingly difficult for his mother to maintain the composure she was working toward, because Herbert was causing her to feel emotions, which were also expressly prohibited, not to mention the fact that he was causing her to feel anger and sorrow, probably the most dangerous of all emotions, for they are the most human; anger and sorrow do not even exist in the Next Level. The harder she tried to ignore herself, the further her frustration extended, until finally her vehicle overflowed with a rage she could no longer contain.

Something horrible has happened. L.D.'s dead. I still can't believe this is happening. His parents found him hanging from a tree in the front yard this morning. I guess someone driving by at 4 a.m. noticed and rang the doorbell. They called an ambulance, but it was too late.

I feel totally numb. I mean, I can't feel anything but hatred. I haven't even been able to cry. How could he do this to me? I'm totally alone now. I have NO ONE. I just need to disappear, I've gotta get out of here. I'll fucking die if I stay, I know this.

I need a release. I need to go. I don't know where. I'll just get out of this. That's it. That's all there is.

ESCAPE

Herbert ran faster than he thought he could run. He wasn't afraid, so he couldn't understand why he was running. Nevertheless, he didn't stop until he reached the highway. He stuck out his thumb.

Rides with families (so strange in their nuclear normalcy, beyond Herbert's comprehension) and truckers (easy to talk to, easy to bullshit) took him as far away as he thought he needed to be.

One day, he arrived in this town called Monkhole. It quickly became his very own promised land and everything he saw became sacred. Herbert was Monkhole's messiah, and vice versa. The place and the man trusted each other pignosedly. Throughout his remaining days, Herbert would stare up at the sky and exchange evil prayers with the land.

No one is sure whether Herbert has lost his mind or if he has always been the way he is. He has his obsessions like every man should, but Herbert's obsessions are weirder than most average, middle-of-the-road obsessions. He has his boredom, and yet he is not a pervert. Biscuits of emotion are rarely seen, scarcely inferred. A life faring sexless as the hairs of a day, which is perhaps why his friend Howard seems to understand him so, although the conditions of the one's solitary confinement differ tremendously from those of his pal.

In the morning, it is always best to be greeted with silence. Herbert looks at the colors in the sky all around him. He thinks of how shitty life is, prays, and goes outside to the cows. *Moo moo*, they greet him. *Yeah, moo yourself,* he caws back. He has his overalls on, the ones his favorite whore says he looks cute in, especially when the ignorant grin on his face sparkles into an insufferable hollow with the alarming suddenness of a dinner bell ringing in the distant corners of someone else's memory.

We know what is inside you, Martin Jones once said to him. *It is the same thing that is inside all of us who have been Chosen to move beyond this burdensome planet. You have a soul inside you, as do all humans. But encased within that soul, there is another soul that glimmers like a diamond, and that sub-soul will be your boarding pass to the Next Level.*

Two of the cows recently had babies. Herbert watches them quite often. He has named the white one "Milkweed," and her spouse, "Martin." Milkweed and Martin's children flock around them. Their rough whiskers rub up against Mama's hide.

By the time Tanya found the Overcomers, she was four months pregnant and lost. L.D. had hung himself the month before and the bean that would become Herbert was beginning to protrude through the center of her dress. She took to the road because she basically had no other option; that is to say, she had come to no firm conclusion when pondering her dilemma. After smoking and fucking her way through junior high school, finally giving up after flunking out of eighth grade three years in a row, she found herself knocked up, without friends, and in violent conflict with her parents. It seemed like an ideal time to fuck off, so she hitchhiked around the country with no fixed destination in mind.

In a short time, barely a month, she had managed to completely separate herself from her past, to the extent that she hardly remembered where she had come from. Whenever she thought back on her old life, she'd circumvent the figures standing throughout the hallway of her memory and devote her thoughts, whether consciously or unconsciously, to the houses-in-construction she and L.D. used to vandalize. They were all based on the same model, bland two-story creatures with oak-colored hardwood floors and cabinets in the kitchen, too many bathrooms and windows, brass doorknobs and brick exteriors with back decks overlooking massive backyards flourishing with forests that were green until autumn arrived and all the leaves died, camouflaging their identities into the pastel landscape of concrete foundations rooted deeply in the soil, until it got colder and everything became a blur, the streets indecipherable from the houses, the forest. You would see deer someone had not yet managed to kill running around back there. Looking out the window and seeing a BMW drive past the Port-A-John situated in the mud of the lot and her nose hurting when she blew smoke out of it. Another house sat across the street, but it was finished being built and someone lives there now. Broken glass in the driveway.

One night, she found herself kicking around a small town in the middle of the desert, staying at the home of some friendly new-age hippies who ran a vegetarian café. They had planned on attending an "alternative religion" event at the town's community center that evening, and asked Tanya if she'd like to come along.

The small audience sat in uncomfortable brown fold-out chairs listening to the presentation being offered by a hypnotically cheery middle-aged man. A few dozen of his followers, his congregation, sat behind him, clothed in white robes, their heads shaved clean.

TRANSMISSION

Good evening. This is a very exciting time for us. Who is "us"? My name is Martin Jones, and sitting behind me are a number of my students, or, in the old words of religious literature, my disciples, who are trying to prepare themselves for the Next Evolutionary Level of Existence, which is synonymous with what Christians refer to as the Kingdom of Heaven. We have come here tonight to speak to you about the most urgent thing on our minds, and what we suspect will be the most urgent thing on the minds of those who will connect with us.

To put it plain and simple, this planet is about to be recycled. Your only chance to survive is to leave with us.

Now, I understand this sounds quite bold in terms of religion, in terms of intelligent thinking even. But intelligent human beings will also recognize the fact that all things have their season—just as there is always a beginning, all things must also come to an end. We see this demonstrated every day before our eyes in nature. Now, we're not saying that planet Earth is coming to an end; we're saying it's about to be recycled, refurbished, spaded under so that it will have another chance to serve as a garden for a future human civilization.

The reason why this is such an exciting time for us is that

we are on the threshold of the end of this civilization. Where will you be found? Who will be the one to judge you?

Some of you are shaking your heads. *Who is this funny-looking old man standing up here, babbling away about the end of the world?* you're probably asking yourselves. *Who does he think he is?* Well, in order to answer that question, I must first tell you who My Father is.

My Father is not a human father. My Father does not belong to this species or to this level of existence. My Father is a member of the Next Level of Existence, the Kingdom of Eternal Life. My Father gave birth to me, long before this civilization began, in the Next Evolutionary Level of Existence.

If you choose not to believe me, that's fine, that's not important to me. Although I wish you would believe it, because those who do will stand a chance of surviving the impending recycling that is about to occur.

No one is here tonight against their will. All of us have chosen to be here. What's more, we have been Chosen to be here by Our Father above. And it is us and us only who will survive long after the current civilization has been recycled. We are here to offer you LIFE for the very first time. And we're not talking about human life, either.

If you've read the Bible, studied any sacred literature, you know that a savior is supposed to come during the last days of civilization to rescue all the devoted—this is supposed to be the return of Jesus Christ. The fact is, "Jesus Christ" is merely the name that was attached to that figure's body or vehicle, in the language of the Next Level. That soul was transported to Earth 2,000 years ago to warn civilization of the impending refurbishment, and that soul has returned to Earth, and is in this room tonight, spreading the message.

Some of you may find it difficult to believe that Christ's mind has been transplanted into this, my vehicle. I must admit it's me. And I am here to teach you what you can do to spare yourself from the impending disaster, just like I did

2,000 years ago. What I am saying tonight I also said then, the same message being transmitted in a newer, more contemporary language.

Now, the planet Earth is about to be recycled. We look at planet Earth as a stepping-stone in the ongoing process science calls Evolution. Just as nature evolves, civilization appears to evolve, as well, under the name of progress. Each segment of civilization has the option to evolve upwards and become more civilized, less barbaric. Sometimes civilization goes the civilized route, which is the way it should go, but at other times, it doesn't. Sometimes, under the guise of "progress," civilization appears to have evolved, when it has actually become more barbaric and quicker to condemn the rest of the world, quicker to kill the parts of the world that don't think the way it thinks.

Now, I just said that I am the return of the Son of my Father. I was dispatched to Earth by the authorities of the Next Level, with whom we are in constant contact. My existence on this planet has been devoted to assisting my students, who were also with me as disciples 2,000 years ago, rid themselves of all human behavior, characteristics, and addictions—all the ties that attempt to bind us to this regressive level of existence. This preparation for entrance into the Next Level we call "the Process," because that's exactly what it is—a process of totally overcoming, severing the ties to our old lives in preparation for the Next Level.

In a book we published not too long ago, entitled *Evacuate Earth!: How the Gates of Eternity May be Entered*, we said there are three types of individuals who will survive the recycling. The first type is the individual who has done the human overcoming I just described, to the extent that the individual is prepared to devote themselves to service in the Next Level of Existence.

When all human attributes have been overcome, you will be a match for a physical body in the New Kingdom. Most of the inhabitants of Earth operate under the idea that we are bound to the flesh, what philosophers have called the corporeal, or the body. Just as there is a human body, the beings in the Next Level also have physical, biological bodies. You see, the Next Level is not just a spiritual place—it's also a physical place.

What does a body from the Next Level look like? You might say it resembles an android or an extraterrestrial. You might even say it resembles the human body in some ways, although the Next Level body is more highly evolved and therefore less animalistic than the human body. It has no need for the same kind of fuel the human body needs, because it exists in a non-Earthly environment.

Imagine a body in the same form as the humanoid body, the same basic design, only with no hair. No teeth are needed for eating, as we fuel our bodies by other means in the Next Level. There are remnants of ears and a nose—what you would call remnants—although they function very well as ears and noses. There is no need for a voice box, as the Next Level beings communicate through thoughts. Also, the skin is different from human skin, more rubbery, because the atmospheric conditions are different from those here on Earth. Another important difference is the fact that there are no genders in the Next Level of Existence. The reason is simple: The Next Level body has a built-in capacity for reproduction. In other words, Next Level beings are capable of reproducing themselves through other means.

That is, in short, what a Representative of the Next Level looks like—quite a far cry from the representations you see of space aliens on TV.

There's an old saying about how some things are born of the flesh and some things are born of the spirit. "Born of water" is synonymous with being born of the flesh, while "born of fire" is synonymous with being born of the spirit. And just as this planet was once flooded by the high forces of the

Next Level, we have been informed that the next cleansing, the next recycling, will be by fire.

How, exactly, will this disaster occur? I can't know all the particulars. Talk to the meteorologists, the people who study volcanoes, the ozone layers. Talk to the people who study the environment. What is the one thing that all these people will tell you? That planet Earth is in trouble.

What's more, look around yourselves. Look at the way that people are unable to restrain themselves nowadays and have no respect for their neighbors whatsoever. They're so unrestrained that if you say something that makes them un-happy, they'll start shooting guns at you. The next thing you know you have a little war in this neighborhood that blos-soms into a bigger war. Look at all the fighting going on in different nations, all over the world. These people are aid-ing the spading under themselves, aren't they? This is repre-sentative of the direction civilization is going in—people are quick to condemn each other. What are the lessons the his-tory books teach us, the lesson that so many continue to ig-nore? Don't condemn others or else you will be condemned yourself.

If people were able to truly understand the sacred litera-ture they read, they would see how the seed of human flesh is literally the negative, the seed of evil, of opposition. The Next Level recognizes this low form of existence, and right-fully knows that it is but a stepping-stone to the Kingdom of Eternal Life.

I'm not trying to say that you are evil because you happen to be cloaked in a human vehicle. I happen to be wearing a human vehicle myself, as are all of my students. But we don't like the fact that we have to wear them. The fact is, these bodies are a part of our current task. The task of overcoming the human kingdom involves the overcoming of human flesh—lust, genetic vibrations, the desire to cling to one's family or home or money or fame or a job—the list goes on and on. We must even work to overcome our religious desires. There is not a single religion on Earth today that truly serves God. All ideologies are corrupted and tainted accounts of man's relationship with the forces of the Next Level.

Ancient religious literature was significant to the rules and laws of its time. Just like the newer religious literature is more significant to our age. What did God say to the people before the Messiah came? That he would send a Savior to lead them out of the human kingdom, knowing that some would be prepared for this transition, others wouldn't.

Well, that Messiah came and after a brief teaching period on this planet, He said, *I will come again.* And here He is. What you are now listening to is a direct transmission from what you may call, for better or for worse, the Kingdom of Heaven.

Today's Christians unanimously ignore the most important teachings of the Messiah. Christ said, *If you want to move into My Father's Kingdom, leave everything behind that belongs to this world and follow Me. Unless you truly despise this world, you will never know the Kingdom of Heaven. You have to cling to Me if you are to enter My Father's House.*

Christians think that Jesus wants them to love their families. *Jesus wants me to be happy. Jesus wants me to be rich and successful. Jesus wants me to live a happy life.*

I don't recall Jesus saying any of these things. When did Jesus say anything about the importance of family values? Jesus addressed His teachings directly to individuals, not families or groups. Jesus said that as an individual, *you* must know that this human world is not for you. If you know this world is not for you, then come with Me. I will nourish you with the knowledge you need from My Father's Kingdom, and together we will overcome ourselves and this horrible life in this burdensome world and enter into that Kingdom.

Remember—this is not a spiritual kingdom, not the traditional picture of Heaven-on-Earth you may have conjured up in your mind, but a physical place. I'll tell you something else quite extraordinary: My Father's Kingdom travels in spacecrafts, some of which are even organic. You think this is ridiculous? Look in the Bible. You will find many references to "clouds of light." They didn't have words like UFOs or spacecrafts back then, did they? The fact is, I was transported to Earth in a flying spacecraft or "cloud of light," just as I ascended 2,000 years ago up into that fire in the sky. These spacecrafts function as work stations for the members of the Next Level. How do I know this? Well, feel free to ask any of these people up here if you need further proof—we are all in contact with the high members of the Next Level on a daily basis. That's right, we receive messages from them all the time . . . How else would these messages be transmitted to us if we weren't receiving them from up above, Our Brethren in the skies?

Once we have completed our task here on Earth, totally overcome all our human attributes, a spacecraft will pick us up to transport us to the Next Level of Existence, where we will begin our new tasks. We have not yet been informed as to whether or not we will all go on board a spacecraft together. But we will definitely leave before the recycling occurs. In other words, we do not know yet whether or not we will be wearing these vehicles when we board the spacecraft. It is possible that we will be required to shed or even destroy these shells we're currently wearing before we are admitted. This will probably be the case, although it is also possible that we will walk on board in our present bodies and then be issued new vehicles for exchange. We know for sure that the Next Level has no use for human bodies. It is possible that our task is to prove how much we despise this world, to the extent that we are willing to destroy everything that remains of our humanness and leave no proof behind of the Next Level's existence.

Either way, we have nothing to be afraid of. We are in safe hands. We can easily leave our present forms, our humanoid selves behind to become that soul, that mind inside us, which will inevitably survive that separation when we make the transition to android form.

Souls are very interesting things. You know, My Father's Kingdom plants souls. When a soul is planted, it becomes the great separator. Because each time a Representative from the Next Level is dispatched to Earth, many souls are planted in human vehicles. Even though a soul is planted in the human vehicle, it is actually planted in the spirit of that vehicle, the spirit being the mind or intelligence of that particular human vehicle. In this way, it is more akin to a sub-soul than what humans have been taught to think of when they hear the word "soul." Does that mean that not everybody has a soul? Well, yes it does. But it also means that anybody can have a soul, anybody who can believe in My Father and the Next Level of Existence. As the separator, that soul helps the individual's mind abort human thinking, human behavior, human evaluation, and replace it with the mind they get from their Representatives from the Next Level. When the original mind has been sufficiently filled with the new mind, then the individual is ready to evolve and will be accepted into the Next Level of Existence.

Now, let me say that all human vehicles, given their current genetic structure, corrupt as it may be, have the potential for possession of a soul, even if they do not possess one at this moment. The fact is, every human plant has at least a little bit of that mind in them, a tiny piece of the Next Level mind. So if there is a human listening to me right now who has the slightest bit of curiosity, who asks themselves, *Is it true what Martin Jones is saying?* then the Next Level crew who is responsible for planting souls will hear that, it will attract their attention, and a soul will be made available for that person. So the deposit of that soul could happen very, very quickly.

One thing we're not going to do is cling to life in these

current vehicles until the battery runs out. We don't care enough about this planet to die for it, and be stuck in a box in the ground for eternity. We don't care enough to be aborted by our present bodies, but we care enough to abort them ourselves to prove to Our Father that we are ready to leave this place and go into His Kingdom for Eternity. And these students of mine can say, *We trust the words that Your Son is speaking, Father. We trust the One you have Chosen to send to rescue us. We trust him so much that we are not afraid to follow Him, to leave our bodies behind and leave this place. We know that wherever we're going is a better place, a step up from where we are today!*

Earlier, I stated that there are three types of individuals who will be eligible for admission to the Next Level of Existence. The first type is those who, like my students, have undergone the process of total overcoming.

The second type of individual may not have reached the level of total overcoming that the Next Level requires, but is still faithful to the cause of breaking away from their present reality. These individuals will continue looking to Me and My Father for strength, and may have to experience life in a civilization yet to come before they are able to gain entry.

The third type of individual simply believes what we say. They will hear our voice at the moment that our task has been completed. They may not know where it's coming from, but they will sense my physical presence in this world and know that I have vacated it. Then they will say to themselves, *I've got to leave this all behind. There is a better place for me, and it is time for me to go there.*

This simple belief that I describe occurred in the mind of the thief who hung on the cross next to Jesus Christ. When Jesus recognized that belief, He said to the thief that day he would, upon their departure, be with Him in Paradise. Jesus knew that the thief honestly believed. And Jesus knew that's all it would take for the thief to make it into Heaven—for him to believe who He was. Believing in Him even when He was being killed as a heretic—against the church, against the system, the dominant ideology of those times.

In a similar fashion, the dominant system of thought is opposed to our view of the world, opposed to the Truth. And the church of today certainly views us as being against the church. But the church of today is not a church of God. The only true church of today is that which has a connection with the present incarnation of the Next Level of Existence, the Kingdom of Eternity, the Kingdom of Heaven, the Kingdom of God, and its Representative.

This is such a joyous time for us, even though we know we are near the end, but that is why it is such an exciting time for us. We don't want to build a church on this planet to leave behind. We don't want a big gothic cathedral. We don't want a membership roll. We don't want to help you reproduce so we can put more children on the Sunday school roll in our church. We are a group of believers in the Next Level of Existence. We want to leave this planet so that we can go and be of service to that Kingdom.

I'm not saying that a strong humanitarian drive is not a healthy thing to have when you're in the human kingdom. Because a strong humanitarian drive is always motivated, ever eager to improve. But you must understand that the condition of being human is just a temporary condition, just a stepping stone in the greater cycle of being. When you are offered an opportunity to get out of this kingdom, you must evaluate and accept this Truth. This is as scientific as you can get, as true as true can be, but you have to know me, you have to trust me, you have to believe in me. There are some of you, in this room tonight, who didn't know me before, but who know me now. I can feel you knowing me. There is something in your head that's saying, *I don't know what it is, but something makes me know that fellow standing up there, and something makes me know that what he is saying is true. I may be wrong, but I am going to find out if I need to be a part of what he's talking about. I don't like the direction the world is going in these days, this Earth is not a place for me, and he is offering me a chance to escape, to go somewhere where I truly belong.*

If you have some of My Father's mind in you, you will recognize us and recognize this information, without a doubt. But I must warn you: Even though you recognize me, the forces of this world will dive in with all the strength they can muster and attempt to make you lose that recognition, make you not trust me, make you come to your senses and return to your service of this world. The lower forces' whole effort is bent on preventing potential members of the Next Level from entering the Kingdom of Heaven.

What you should know is that the lower forces, who control human civilization using a complex network of tools—the media, religion, schools, the list could go on and on, extending to every level of society—these lower forces have used these tools to genetically program the human body to reject this information. Indeed, upon our departure, this information, the Truth, will completely vanish from the atmosphere.

Those who are religious-minded might look at me and say, *This is the Anti-Christ! This is the Spurious Messiah that I've been warned about!* (For those of you who don't know, the term "Spurious Messiah" has been used by many religious leaders who think that a false messiah will arrive on Earth before Christ's second coming in an effort to deter His potential followers.) Well, I hate to tell you, but the Anti-Christ has been present on this planet ever since my departure 2,000 years ago. And his followers have done everything they can, through religion, government, "acceptable" morality, through concepts like "human responsibility," to brainwash humans into expecting "Heaven on Earth." These evil forces have brainwashed humans, especially modern day Christians, to look at our arrival on Earth as the Anti-Christ. Those evil forces, who are essentially humanoid space aliens, the Opposition, have programmed humans into preparing for the future by having children, saving money so their children can have a future, so that their children's children can have a future . . . A future in what? The human kingdom? What a horrendous abomination! In actuality, anyone who is planning on staying on Earth is in fact investing everything in the Anti-Christ—a Spurious Messiah indeed!

Tonight, we are merely asking you to ask yourself a question: Are you ready for Eternal Life in another physical realm? Are you able to accept the Pure Truth, untainted by the evil forces this planet has fallen into the hands of?

Only you can know if you have been Chosen. For those of you who are still uncertain, I hope you will at least ponder this. Remember: This is an individual decision for you to make, so don't ask your neighbors, your friends, or your family what they think of all this. As soon as you tell anyone else, they will most likely be used as instruments by the lower forces to make you disbelieve, to make you remain on Earth in expectancy of their false conception of Heaven, which is ultimately death.

Instead, go into the privacy of your "closet," the deepest pocket of your mind, and see if you can channel the purest, highest source that you might consider to be God, and ask: *What about this? Is this information for real? Is this meant for me? If it is, please give me the strength I need to act on it.*

I guarantee you will hear these words again.

We hope to be of service to you in the time before our departure from this planet. Our thoughts will be of you. We hope your thoughts will be of Our Father's Kingdom.

ESCAPE

(CONTINUED)

At the bottom of the hill, there is a large oak tree under which a few of the cows congregate, sitting and flipping their tails. Herbert stares at them for a little while. *Must want to get out of the sun*, Herbert thinks to himself. He sniffles his nose. Suddenly, he exhales roughly through his nostrils, shooting out a tunnel of snot onto the back of his hand. He studies the sleek green liquid, noticing a tiny hardened particle sticking out, like an island in the middle of a lake. He picks the booger out and plops it in his mouth, wiping the rest of the river on the side of his overalls.

One of the cows, Gigi, her enormous titty brushing up against the ground, moves her head to the side, an ear along with it. She shrugs to herself as she chews on some cud, wondering about the length of her days. Herbert blows some more snotty boogers out. A frequent occurrence: As he sits on the field, a bug feeding on stale milk will fly up into his nostrils, biting the inside of his nose. He'll squish it, blow the dead bug's guts and some blood out, watch as it lands on the Lord's turf.

A baby cow has a disease. She is skinny, diarrhetic, and in-fested with a weird sort of bug that swarms around her night and day. Herbert glances at her as he takes out an apple, wipes it off with his spanking unused snot rag, takes a bite. It is quite fresh and green. As he swallows, he watches a giant turd fall to the ground. Herbert burps and puts a weed in his mouth to provide a sort of oniony contrast to the taste of the apple.

Shortly after his arrival in Monkhole, Herbert moved into an abandoned farmhouse. He kept his cows down the street, behind a few acres of fenced-in land with a tiny barn on top of a hill.

Herbert would milk his cows, but he doesn't care about milking a profit off of them. They are there for companionship, nothing else. Hot milk hits the ground, splattering upwards to the udders. Soon the field began to smell wan as the cow shit rotted beneath the sun upon a dead grass layer of spoilt milk. Both cows and Herbert have grown immune to the stench, nobody ever comes around, so after performing his single daily chore, he is free to wallow about in the stinky field.

Herbert never does more than the cows do. He sits. He wanders about. Watches them. Half the time, he realizes, they aren't even aware of his presence.

All the edges of Herbert's "new" life have been filtered through the eyes of these gods. The cows are under his command. He's their leader, even though he probably doesn't care. In fact, he doesn't. He is a reluctant god. He's their ruler whether he likes it or not.

The ultimate ending was the day he woke up to realize it no longer mattered to him. The whole program he had been born into, the "highest" alternative, all its efforts to sever itself from Earth's institutions—the governments that kill, the religions that chain humans to death and destruction, the media with its obsession with scandal, the Opposition's breeding ground for lies. None of it for him. There was nothing to Overcome because he had never been a part of it all to begin with. The Overcomers channeled their daily energies into this critique of institutional existence, but the only institution that existed for Herbert was the Overcomers and their Next Level.

He started fucking his mother because he wasn't capable of penetrating her in any other way—they weren't allowed to discuss anything apart from Overcoming, he wasn't allowed to seek answers to the questions that had been popping up in his brain. So he decided to look elsewhere, to run away from the self he no longer trusted, no longer believed in, abandoning all his youthful aspirations . . .

He once believed he'd been Chosen. He once believed that his strength in spirit and his abstinence from life outside would reap the highest rewards upon attaining the Next Level. But he had already been through the whole process, he had already neutralized his entire being throughout the course of his first eighteen years on the planet.

This, his new life in Monkhole, is the Next Level, the destination he had been taught to perceive, the landscape before him as achromatic as the soul he left behind.

Nous avons vu des astres
Et des flots; nous avons vu des sables aussi;
Et, malgré bien des chocs et d'imprévus désastres,
Nous nous sommes souvent ennuyés, comme ici.

—Charles Baudelaire, "Le voyage"

FRIENDS

Howard, Ruphis, and Herbert are friends. One day, they embark on a journey to the whorehouse in the next town. Herbert shoots his load into the face of a one-armed saint, smiles, farts, and goes away. Ruphis jerks his big wide meat back and forth, occasionally slapping the whore he's fucking in the face with it, then sticks it back inside, pumps a little harder, pulls out, shoots, and frowns. Howard likes having two girls at the same time, one to lick his ass while the other munches on his balls. After eating his ass out for about an hour, she lets him fuck her without a condom while the other one continues to lick his balls off. Afterwards, the whore stands over the bidet by the window, washing her cunt while the sun shines in between her legs. Her sister, the scrotum sucker, slips on a pair of sunglasses.

Ruphis and Herbert stand in a field.

Ruphis and Herbert argue.

Ruphis is wearing a tie-dyed doo-rag on his skull, while a thin line of titsnot hangs off Herbert's chin.

Herbert is milking a cow, you see.

Ruphis chooses not to inform Herbert of the fishwire of titsnot drooping lustily southward as though responding to the masculine urges of gravity.

Ruphis and Herbert are too involved with this argument, each perplexed by the other's idleness or stupidity or indifference.

What they're arguing about now, I don't recall, but it's not important anyway.

All the shouting frightens Gigi the cow. She wags her tail and walks away.

None of the cows fuck on sunny days. It is not improbable that they find some sort of fault with pleasant weather, preferring the moistness of the ground to dig their paws into, so to speak, when committing that carnal sin we shall attempt to remain silent about for these remaining pages.

At one point in the argument, Ruphis claims Herbert is a liar and will never be able to overcome his seemingly automatic inclination toward evasiveness.

Herbert's at a loss for words, so he pulls out his dick and pisses on Ruphis.

Ruphis screams like a woman.

A worm below his feet senses his fear as a trickle of piss soaks through the ground, stinging its skin. It slugs through a sticky dirt tunnel in order to escape the piss. Some worms eat wet leaves. Others just eat themselves. Have you ever seen a worm use the bathroom? I haven't. But I'm quite curious as to how they do it. I'm sure they have to excrete somehow, just like any other man, animal, fetus. The worm is made out of mucous membranes. In some countries, they eat them. They must taste salty.

The worm drowns in Herbert's pee.

You asshole! screams Ruphis. *I can't believe you just pissed on me!*

He picks up a bucket, which, now empty, was once filled with milk, all the same: hits Herbert in the side of the head. Herbert falls down, stunned. He lapses into a momentary daze during which he can see the sky gluing itself together. Shadows where there are none, a brown cow licking its lips. The sun's white stare threatening to burn out his retinas. Slowly, as if on cue, a thick cloud begins to eclipse the light. God drops the remote control on the hardwood floor; batteries pop out; world goes on.

Later, they are somehow able to laugh off their little disagreement, Herbert with a large welt on the side of his head, Ruphis in his piss-stained clothing. They walk off into the dusk like the headdress of a naked Indian woman, one arm wrapped around the other's shoulder, Friends For Life. They go into the nearby town to eat french fries at a diner. Their conversation resembles a rampant foray into pastime obligation. If either one smoked, they could light cigarettes at such a moment and the conversation would become more reminiscent. But alas, neither of the pair is interesting enough to smoke.

Sitting in the next booth over, a young couple eats in silence as they attempt to maintain control of their rowdy, hyperactive children. It can only be hoped that they will one day soon give in to the protocol forces of birth control.

Splitting apart the length of Ruphis's and Herbert's conversation, a baby's arm reaches down and pulls Herbert's hair, causing Herbert to scream not quite as loud as Ruphis had earlier in the day but perhaps a bit louder than Bliff did when the metal flew into his eyes. The couple apologize profusely for their little lamb's behavior, and proffer the gesture of scolding the brat in front of Herbert. Although he claims he doesn't care, Ruphis senses something brewing deep within.

Soon after, they pay their bill and leave the restaurant. And it is indeed then that the tears break through just like Ruphis had predicted, as they walk silently through the dark.

Oh, why did that baby have to pull my hairs out? he cries. *They took me so long to grow!*

Don't hate yourself, Herbert, his dear piss-stained friend swiftly opines. *There's always the day after tomorrow.*

There should be a religion based upon that principle, Herbert sniffles.

If I was the leader of a church, the whole world would be damned.

Ruphis knows this comment will have a soothing effect on Herbert's state of mind. There is nothing left to say, so off they walk into the white noise of the dying day, Ruphis with his beloved doo-rag scotch-taped to his head, Herbert with a trace of titsnot still hanging down off his chin toward the devil.

THE JOURNEY

Herbert and I decided to go into the next town over in order to find some juice. Well, sure, they sell juice at the store in Monkhole. But their selection is rather limited, in my opinion. I crave authenticity when it comes to my juices. For this reason, I suppose I'm some sort of intellectual. My favorite flavors are strawberry-kiwi, orange, apple, and carrot. Strawberry-kiwi is definitely Number One on the list. It is so good and it stains like blood or wine. But you have to buy a lot to make it last, because it starts to get old and too sweet after a while. In case you don't know, strawberry-kiwi is a sickly color. A pink so pale it looks as if the juice were dying or something. I went crazy one summer and drank too much of it. I ended up vomiting. As it came up, it sort of tasted like poisoned tomatoes. I think I puked it because the batch I drank had been sitting in the refrigerator for too long and had gone bad. I knew this the second I put it in my mouth, as all the sugars had floated up to the top where they lazed upon the surface like bugs in a lake, creating a filmy residue. Thus, it was overly sweet instead of sour; had it been sour, I would have immediately known to stay away from and dispose of it as swiftly as possible. For sure, it never would have been consumed.

I don't know much about the nutritional value of these

specially manufactured flavors. I realize that strawberry-kiwi is not completely natural, as the two fruits usually don't go together. I'm not even sure if they're able to grow in the same climate. I'm not always sure which juices are Natural and which are From Concentrate. Actually, I don't even know what Concentrate means. I don't know much about fruits. Strawberry and kiwi. But I suppose this doesn't really matter, since the juices I'm drinking aren't authentic, but rather imitative. They're flavors—the recreation of what these two fruits are supposedly like, but aren't actually, in nature; what is actually the chemical synthesis of a flavor I like all the same even if I'm so far removed from what the real thing happens to be or not to be. Occasionally, I'll go overboard and buy grape. But it's usually not my sort of thing. (I hear it's good for you if you're sick.)

Herbert moved here three years ago. Up until then, my life had been pretty empty. I moved here to . . . get away from myself, so to speak. Herbert came here in his lifelong quest for boredom. The one thing we had in common is that we both knew what we were looking for, and we knew that we were looking for things that couldn't be found.

I settled into a tiny patched villa that was situated on the edge of a cliff. The man living there before me hadn't taken very good care of it, nor himself, for that matter. I was referred to him by a mutual acquaintance, and as I approached the tiny palace, which was in such bad condition that it seemed to have devolved into a shack (I say "devolved" because it is clear that it was probably once something, something sturdy, and had fallen into such disrepair that you could not really brand it as anything but shit, a word Grandma told me never to say, but I say it anyway when I'm angry, or when I need to describe certain things, such as the house I'm living in), a distinctive waft began to penetrate my senses. It wasn't pleasant, to say the least, and it lingered mysteriously all around the surrounding area. I had no doubt in my mind that this house in front of me, the house I had come to possibly purchase, was the source of this breeze. But I did have doubts about the whole scene in general. You know, like whether this house should be lived in or destroyed. Eventually, I realized I didn't care, and I found myself knocking on the front door.

Well, this is it, the guy said immodestly as he led me in. He was an older, balding man, about fifty-six pounds overweight. He was wearing stained white tennis shorts and a white undershirt, and I noticed what looked like cigar burns going up and down his arms.

The floor was made of softwood. It was all scratched up, and it looked as though it hadn't been mopped in years, or even a decade. The house—more like a cabin—consisted of one room with a bed against the right wall, a small kitchen facility in the corner, and a bunch of trash laying everywhere else. There was no furniture to speak of, not even a table, so I'm assuming the guy probably ate off the floor. No bathroom, no closet; lots of stink, lots of rot.

He led me out back through the screen door. There were two rusty yard chairs on the back porch; he offered me a seat and we sat there, staring off the edge of the mountain at the yards of empty space below us. I was entranced, I could hardly speak. I could see myself falling quite easily. Or if an earthquake were to occur, the entire cabin, so tiny and insignificant in proportion to the void down below, would crumble and fall right off the edge along with centuries of stale sedimentary rock.

I told him I'd take it.

He asked me how much of Monkhole I had seen thus far. Not a whole lot. He offered to drive me around and point stuff out. I accepted.

We climbed into his beat-up blue pickup truck and drove away from the edge. He showed me the store. The school-house. He pointed out some cows. There were a few similar-looking villas randomly scattered about here and there, as sporadic as the candy wrappers and open bottles on the floor of the cabin. Mostly, it was just open space.

He sold me the place for almost nothing and disappeared. I have no idea where he went. Maybe he got into his truck with all his trash and drove off the edge of the cliff. He took the strange smell with him.

Not long after I moved in, I had a birthday party. Herbert was there; he had long gray hairs at the time that remind me of my grandmother in the coffin. I didn't know who Herbert was. Only that, in his loneliness, he had come to celebrate my birthday with me. Problem is, he was the only one at the party. I didn't know anyone in Monkhole at the time. Nonetheless, I had sent out a bunch of invitations anyway, but they turned out to have the wrong date on them. So there was this big mystery of how Herbert had gotten there without anyone else, considering the fact that I had no idea who or what he was. I didn't ask any questions because I didn't want to be rude, and pretty soon I knew him quite well. He never did leave my villa that night. Sometimes I wonder if he's still in here with me.

Grandma gave me her telescope when she got kicked out of the navy. I guess she was afraid that something would happen if we left her all alone with it. In the coffin, her corpse resembled a dead spider. Herbert came with me to the funeral, to show his support. In his sermon, the preacher said that she had acquired a gift for the overall, and perhaps I (her only surviving relative) would be lucky enough to inherit it, along with a couple of other virtues. Midway through the service, Herbert turned to me and whispered in my ear, *I'm the one who killed her, Ruphis.*

At the time of her death, Grandma was beginning to look like a dodgy old man. I can still hear her moaning in the background of my thoughts. *Listen to the music inside your head, Ruphis,* she once said to me. *If you're scared at night, it will save you.*

Then Herbert came along and it seemed that I no longer needed to be saved. I suddenly had something else . . . something I am not brave enough to name. I think she could've done something better with her life, or at least died a more dignified death, immolated herself, for example.

The night she died, Herbert and I had gone to visit her. When we arrived, we knocked on the door, and there was no answer. I tried the knob; it was unlocked, so we opened it and walked in. We found her in the corner of the living room in a rocking chair with a shotgun sticking out of her mouth, rocking back and forth to the rhythm of the shadows she was creating on the floor all around her. She had a fire lit in the fireplace, so we put it out, wrapped a blanket around her, said *Goodnight, Grandma*, that was that. The next morning, we found her with the telescope shoved up her cunt. The barrel of the shotgun had been unloaded in her jaw. I figured she had done this to herself. It never occurred to me that Herbert got up in the middle of the night to perform this task—it seemed too . . . strenuous, or something. But then at the funeral, when he told me he killed her, I didn't really care. My only hope is that she got one last glance at the stars before it happened, because I know for a fact that she doesn't get to see them now.

As we rounded the corner of an abandoned apartment building in town, we heard a cat meowing in the distance. This frightened Herbert out of his cold drawn-out wits, and he immediately fell down some stairs. It was dark down there so I couldn't see him all too well. *Herbert*, I cried out, laughing. Herbert wasn't all right. I knew this for a fact cos usually when Herbert fell, he would laugh about it immediately afterwards, trying to cover up his mistake with a bandage on his knee. All at once, I realized what may be sterilely referred to as the truth of the moment, it felt like a hammer cracking down upon my head: Herbert had fallen down on purpose.

I'm ready to go flying off some mountain so my dead bones can land in some alleyway that human life has abandoned. I shout at the jesus martians who are abandoning shelter as I fucking screw myself into another world. I don't care that I smell or I abandoned my religion. I bleed from my chin. My greatest fear is the evil goats I see in my dream, the possibility they will turn out to be real, are being raised on a goat farm in some small town twenty miles west of here. For a cracker, I am a very needy person. I.e., I use people. Because people, to me, are like cows, ridiculously shitting away at some gay farm in the next town over. Sweet Jesus is on the microphone singing the starlight express. A change of mind blows in with the wind, I swallow too much of it and vomit. Loose-ended kids sitting in a diner smoking cigarettes will never know what happened. Ugly virtue my negligent name. Fuck the pseudo-nature of last year's existence. Here comes someone through the doorway, another year to drive a screwdriver through. The rotting garbage leaking out of the bin in the corner has a Bible sitting on top of it. My hairy dot happens to have a reality of its own. I begin to light my skin on fire in a vain attempt to prove something about my fate. Nothing's working. I say a prayer and it bounces right off the ceiling. I take a knife and try to swallow it. The penal victory an inane game. The teenager lights another cig. Not happy with coloring it all out. Distractions cost one cent each. A sharp object sticking out of my eyeball the only thing I am capable of feeling. One always gets abandoned after sex. Thus, it is always best to be drunk when you are getting fucked. Rub my itchy dick against bitch's face. See if Grandma likes the sweaty abuse I performed on Barbie doll ceramics in that summer of my childhood. She needed to suck on the cinema of my taste, but creed is more important than vice. Don't get a thick rise out of me. Fear of abandonment is crucial for a furry animal. Besides, if Abraham Lincoln was really up my ass for that long, maybe Nancy can get a free suck off the camel's thong. But enough about the high politics of heaven for now. Those who came here sensing utopic proprieties deserve to get the lost master beat out of them.

Now you know I am ready for some soft justifications. Limit me, baby. Limit me all night long. For an eternity, the sordid ugliness, when it's dark, you're always alone. Magic man glistens on the table, burned and low. A Turkish delight all I may see. Red radicality more grand than thou, who beckons. Words become too obscure to cohere. We think only sideways. We cork open our box of fears, see through the glass and see through the wood. Red lives inhere. There is a time for answers. The heat from those cigarette butts reminds me of an organ for some reason. Perhaps it is the windy rain. The pickup truck rests motionless in the lot. Teenagers stare at it and ponder. Grunt lewd absurdities in deep voices. All may be almost clear, clear as the wood on these tables. I have turned into a lonely Jew. I stare at the flowers on the floor and try to imagine what they would look like with their petals missing. One day, I will get killed amongst the violence of all this open space.

HOWARD BLEEDS

Howard began his day by bleeding. Upon waking, he noticed a huge gash on the side of his forehead with blood leaking out of it. *How did that happen?* he impassively wondered.

Things like this would often happen at night while Howard slept alone in his cabin. He was the sole inhabitant of a rather vast parcel of land outside of Monkhole, beyond the next town over, in unnamed territory. The cabin had been built in the middle of the forest. It is impossible to determine when Howard first arrived there. He seemed to have organically sprouted, that was that. Perhaps he had been there since the beginning of time. Who knows?

He opened up the cabinet and removed a small bandage. Then he turned to stare at himself in the mirror, studying the lines that had arisen on his face. His face was fair, his hairline a bit asymmetrical, largely uneventful. He had spent much of his life attempting to cover his face with hair, but when patches of his beard began falling off for no apparent reason, he decided it might be best to remove it himself, disallowing nature to follow her rapturous course. As he raised the edge of the razor toward the side of his face, he noticed his bandaged head once more. He then proceeded to eradicate the rough fuzz that had grown during the night. The minuscule hairs fell down into the sink. Some of them got stuck between folds in the razor, and were to be flushed away by the force of running water.

The table lay in the center of the cabin, and this is where he sat, eating his breakfast, drifting in and out of an early morning daze, which he wouldn't emerge from until much later in the day, when Ruphis arrived for tea and chat. *I don't know what to do with myself*, he pensively embellished. *Maybe I should just lie and die.*

These recent mysterious physical injuries occurring solely in states of nocturne had ceased to intrigue him. He was unable to pinpoint a cause, as throughout his life he had always been a relatively calm, heavy sleeper, no history of mischievous nighttime deeds, sleepwalking, or dirty dreams. He slept so heavily that, oftentimes, he forgot to dream altogether. Or if he did dream, then he'd have no memory of the dream's content upon waking. But he enjoyed sleep. The cool morning air always signified hostility to Howard's habitation; if unconsciousness would somehow allow him to avoid it, he would do so at all costs. As soon as that annoying brightness had shone its rays through the window above his bed, he knew that it would linger inside him for the rest of the day, temporarily interrupting the sweet righteous sensation of his body's discharge into nothingness.

Sleep provided a sort of entrance into dangerous territories. Howard's navigation skills were, sad to say, lacking. He knew nothing *à ce propos*; he had never read Mr. Freud or Mr. Jung; therefore, he stayed asleep as often as he could. Howard lived based on the intuition that his life didn't pass quite so slowly when he was asleep. Thus, the pros and cons having been weighed long ago, the conclusion has been drawn that it is altogether worth getting banged up while his vision disappeared. (Perhaps even fun and charming. Or somehow significant.)

Every morning, instead of eating breakfast, Howard did an elaborate meditation, placing him in the precarious position of having both legs wrapped around his neck at sunrise, his neck on the verge of snapping. Afterwards, he'd sit in front of the typewriter in the center of the cabin and commence work on his latest masterpiece. This was daily routine. He had been performing these tasks day after day, for years on end. He no longer kept track of time and had no idea what year it was. It could've been the seventeenth century, it could've been tomorrow. Such steadiness had led Howard to the penultimate programming of his interiority, which tended to be as diligent as a clock tower in some foreign country: one silent motion leading to the next, a finger scratching a welt beneath the left eye, a beverage consumed, dust collecting on the shelves . . .

The cabin's interior was furnished with an immense quantity of leather-bound volumes. After a strict diet of stealthy production, it had come to pass that Howard was the author of over a hundred literary works that surrounded him as he sat in the center of the room, thinking, typing. He would finish one book and immediately move on to the next. Sometimes he'd type out the last word of a work, roll a blank sheet into the typewriter, and recommence typing without even pausing to assume another stance, already at work on the next opus. Conscious rest didn't matter at all. When his eyes were open, he wanted his brains in constant motion. Sleep would take care of the consequences, he reasoned. Such nihilistic indulgence oftentimes had the adverse effect of inducing a state of euphoric freedom.

Despite his gross output as an artist, it must be admitted that not a single person had ever read one of his books. He had made one attempt in his life to find a publisher, who had returned his manuscript, *Lifestyle Recommendations*, with a confused note explaining the impossibility of marketing such a work which seemed unable to fit into any category, was it literature, was it a self-help manual, was it philosophy, was it a travel guide . . . It exuded qualities of all these categories, and at least a hundred more which I am too tired to name, into a disorganized mass of obtuse sentiments expressed half-sincerely and half-mechanically. Howard brushed this rejection off like a shabby bum might flick a piece of dirt or dandruff off his shoulder, deciding that it was unnecessary for a writer to have readers anyhow; what mattered was the work.

One particular morning, Howard found himself lost. He was working on his most ambitious project to date, a study on victimology. While much fact and fictional speculation had been spilled onto the criminal's visage, the perpetrator of the painful act, the performer of various abuses emotional and real, no one had yet been brave enough to attack the guilt of the victim, who was often forgotten about in the subsequent romance of trial and error. In order for a crime to be committed, there need be a victim. A loser. It seems a preordained role that some people are simply born into, like royalty. Just as the predator seeks a victim, the victim also seeks a predator. Realizing the undeniable facts of life, that someone is always having something taken away from them, removed, or a wound, an infliction of pain (whether real or imagined, depending on the internal problematics [i.e., neuroses] of said victim, which can often deflect the respective victim's perception of what did or did not transpire on the set of the crime), Howard began to register every human being he saw as either a victim or a non-victim (this is insignificant, as Howard never saw anyone). The victim denotes himself in the open revelation of the presence of a certain hunger; he yearns for something real—the simple banality of an encounter. A real encounter as opposed to all the fake, imaginary ones he's conjured up in his mind. This is the same hunger that is felt by the predator on the day he steps outside, intending to quench this hunger via victimization. This hunger unites the two in a dance, or a narrative, that climaxes with the final act, the orgasm of . . . death?

This book would utilize as fodder famous victims, commencing with the figure of Jesus Christ (whose name, too obvious, was being changed by its author to something a little more subtle and quotidian and modern: Martin Jones), moving throughout history to more abstract figures (friends real and imagined, i.e., Herbert and Ruphis), culminating with a figure supposed to represent the modern-day genius (a concept which will be later destroyed).

The starting point: Although the term "victim" only gains significance within specific contexts, the central metaphor that binds all victims together is that of death, or at least the threat thereof. Yes, death. Undeniably so. Howard himself felt that death was insignificant, a tiny pill in a bottle that everyone had (should have) access to . . . There's the will, which takes on primary significance, the will to be victimized, the leaning toward that tower. I mean, we can't deny the presence of desire. Or can we?

The more he pondered, the further away his thoughts ran from him. Such, he furtively reasoned, are the ways of artistry. He was almost pleased when reality came knocking on his door, rescuing us all from that boring maze of literary endeavor.

Come in, Ruphis, he shouted to the fist outside.

Ruphis stood in the doorway, peering into the cobwebs that surrounded him.

Jeez, Howard. When are you going to fix this place up?

Ruphis sat himself down at the breakfast table and wondered about tea.

What are you working on now? he offered.

Oh, just the same, replied Howard, who was so uncommitted he couldn't even talk.

Howard was oftentimes distracted by his own incoherence.

Ruphis, however, was intrigued, then uninterested, then complacent in his disinterestedness (the latter came rather sudden).

Howard . . . began Ruphis.

. . . Yes? Howard anticipatorily replied.

Nothing, it's just . . .

Well, what is it then? I don't have all day, you know.

I'm sorry. I just didn't know how to bring such a tender subject up. But I shall be brave, braver than I have ever been: I was wondering what you thought about the Small.

At that, Howard pushed away his typewriter and grabbed his chin, somehow fully understanding his friend's mysterious inquiry. He took his glasses off and wiped his forehead. A slight pause concurred with the serious contemplation the author undertook in considering the question he was being forced. Then he promptly stood up, performed a tiny kick-dance around the kitchen, pulled down his pants, shoved a yellow cucumber up his ass, fell on the floor, crawled on his hands and knees over to that table in the center of the cabin where Ruphis sat, picked up his glasses off the table, slipped them over his eyes, and declared:

I suppose the small inhabit a certain world that is very separate from the one that we supposedly inhabit at this point in time. Very separate, indeed, from history, even, or at least the way it's been written. But things will always change.

Things changing? Like sprinkling garlic onto a piece of bread?

I don't know. Maybe.

Howard slurred a partial sigh. Then, changing directions slightly:

I really like the books I write because there is a lot of narration in them. Narration is an important tool for an author.

Ruphis was very good at pretending to seem interested in the places that Howard went. Howard never anticipated any commentary on his ideas, and had in fact never even offered Ruphis an opportunity to read his work. Poor Ruphis was thus cast in the darkness of the rest of the world, shielded from the unknowable talents of the gargantuan scribe. But that's okay because Ruphis was illiterate.

Ruphis ventured an invaluable suggestion: *When you are writing a book, don't forget about plot. But back to the subject of the small. Today, I was walking to town with Herbert in order to buy some juice, cos we had run out and I just can't stand the Monkhole kind. So there we are in the store. We made our way to the juice aisle and selected the kinds that we like. I took three quarts of strawberry-kiwi and Herbert got some beer. At the last minute, I decided I might like some carrot juice, as well. So I picked up a liter of that, and we made our way to the check-out line.*

We were standing there and no clerk was around. Nevertheless, the line of people was moving pretty rapidly. I wondered how people were paying for their groceries, bagging them, and leaving the store so quickly, since nobody was behind the counter to assist them. Eventually, it came to be our turn to pay. So we step up and put our juices down on the counter. It was then that I saw him. There was, in fact, a store employee who was whipping those groceries down the conveyor belt, entering digits into the cash register, collecting money, and giving change. He was the size of my finger, Howard, and he was sitting on the edge of the cash register.

Ruphis paused in his story, half-expecting some sort of response from Howard at this richly emotional point.

Instead, Howard stood up silently, walked over to the kitchen area of his cabin, and began making preparations for the tea they were about to sip.

Ruphis, haunted by the image of a ghost he once saw, offered up sacred stories to all who would listen. Thought that by wandering through life, he would eventually find something, a little girl's ass, a cure for his boredom. His grandmother had caught him with his tongue up a five-year-old's pussy a year before she died. Although she didn't really understand what was going on, she could smell trouble brewing in the winds. She got rid of the brat as fast as she could and gave her a candy bar as collateral for her secret, soon after throwing Ruphis out of her home. These games were typical for him. When he was seven, little Loretta Woodrow with whom he played had showed him her flat chest, which was just like his, a little paler perhaps. Ever since that day, he's wanted to lick, yet as he grew older, seldom and seldom had an opportunity come knocking at his door, that blank wall of beauty. There was the occasional Girl Scout selling cookies and other sweet things, but he had to make sure Grandma was away from the house for a while.

Grandma, he asked her one day when he was but a little, insignificant thing, *why do I live with you?*

He knew he had a daddy somewhere in that big bad world, but he had never heard of a mother.

Gruff Grandma grunted and sniffed her armpit. *Well, let me tell you something. You won't remember your daddy, cos you ain't seen him since you was a baby. But he was a bad, bad man.*

She stopped suddenly and took in some air.

Why was he so bad, Grannie?

Grandma took out the Bible and started to go into a trance as she rocked back and forth in her old rocking chair.

Lord. Please forgive me, said she as her eyes rolled into the back of her head, never to be seen again.

She went on to describe the sordid lifelong misadventure that lived in the person of Ruphis Sr.

Ruphis had been a Grade A low-life from the very beginning. His own mother wouldn't even have anything to do with him. In the town where he grew up, where Ruphis Jr.'s grandmother had lived her whole life, he spent much of his time toiling with the law, as if he owned it. Or had some special access to it that the rest of us didn't. This is what he thought. Not that the laws didn't apply to him, but that he somehow embodied them. He'd drive around town with his mama's shotgun and blast off people's mailboxes. One day, still a teen, he got into his mother's car and started driving. When they finally caught up with him a few years later, he was no longer a teen and there was a kid in the passenger seat. The kid was Ruphis Jr., the veracity of that

"Jr." being questionable. There was also a gun. Drugs. Money. A lot of it.

Ruphis Sr. was taken away, never to be heard from again in-the-flesh. Everything that happened in between, it was up to Ruphis to recall—his first years of life remained a mystery.

Wait a minute. Are midgets even allowed to work these days? Howard pawed his chin and sipped some tea.

That's a good question. I'm not really sure. I don't see how they could, actually. They lack something, y'know? Protein. And they could seriously end up injuring themselves, or someone else. Sometimes I have this really scary dream. There's this hamburger factory. A midget is operating the meat grinder. He has to stand on a stool in order to reach the lever. One day, he accidentally leans over too far and falls in, annihilating himself forever. My dream always ends in a restaurant. I'm sitting there, staring out the window, thinking to myself. The waitress brings me the hamburger I ordered. I lift it up to my face and open my mouth, waking up right before I bite into it.

I don't know, says Howard. *I guess if you think about things too often, those things will eventually pop into your face and scare the living shit out of you.*

At times like these, Howard was glad he didn't have dreams.

Ruphis began to cry. He didn't really know why he was there, but he knew something all the same.

They continued to drink their tea in a silence invented.

Howard speculated that if there existed a precise medium between pure pain and pure pleasure, that moment surely embodied that place.

Ruphis's tears fell away as he turned into an open stare.

Later, Ruphis suggested they leave the house, get some exercise. Howard reluctantly agreed and put his hat on. Eventually, after having slowly walked the length of the forest, they reached the beginning of the dirt-road highway and decided not to stop. They kept going until they reached a hot dog stand parked on the side of a stop-sign intersection.

Victims

Behind the roasting wieners sat their merchant: bearded, Asian, and two feet tall.

Dazed by the vision, Howard said, *I thought midgets weren't allowed to work.*

Ruphis just burst into tears.

When Howard's not writing or getting hurt in his dreams, he likes to bang his head. He has experimented with various household objects—he likes the way it pings when he uses a pot. Sometimes he sees fantastic colors—colors never seen in nature—when he uses a hammer. The photograph of his mother, now dead, is probably Howard's favorite thing to bang his head with because, like other writers, he is impartial to nostalgia.

If you were to ask him *why* he keeps banging his head with these sentimental objects, he probably wouldn't answer you. Howard doesn't talk that often. He wears his silence like a bathrobe, shielding himself from the chills of naked innocence. On his feet are slippers with bunny ears and tails.

The reason: He has a profound envy of the retarded. Perhaps if he succeeds in joining them, he will finally be able to know something.

Howard is a dumbfuck and a failure. Maybe. But if he's stupid, then I guess he's also a genius. In truth, I don't have much time to live my own life because I am always with him, trapped inside him, breathing through his thoughts. I mean, I was never allowed to establish a physical relationship with him, so I just sort of invaded him instead. It's so refreshing to melt into someone you don't even know. You get to live their reality while ignoring your own.

Amidst this chronic administration of self-induced invalidation, Howard was growing increasingly obsessed with the life of his so-called friend Herbert. Howard spied on Herbert, who seemed to do nothing but watch over his cows like God. Howard, in turn, changed the structure of his book and started basing the central character of *Victimology*, which was taking the shape of a long parable, on Herbert. But he did it by reducing Herbert to merely a sketch, practically nothing, thus annihilating him.

Herbert epitomized the victim, due to his disheveled silent oblivion. The gratuitous idiosyncrasies of his person yielded a present absence in their detachment from each other and from Herbert's core, if he had a core, one that was hidden deep beneath a thick surface of pause and empty regard. Herbert's distance exemplified Howard's thesis, it was everything Howard had wanted to express yet there were no words that could adequately express it, debunking the utter wordlessness of his illusory project as a sort of latchkey into that world of lived impossibility that Herbert inhabited. This is why Herbert was unable to separate himself from the land. He had total freedom, having rid his mind of all conceptual structures, leaving no foundation for a unified perception of reality. Any sort of relationship with Herbert was impossible, as he was technically never there, but always somewhere else. Inside, maybe.

But I am also Howard's victim and he is mine. We are two equilateral objects skidding the surface of the page. Paper weights, really.

PERFECT STRANGERS

Howard, Ruphis, and Herbert are seated round the table in Howard's cabin.

Herbert seems to look at Ruphis, but Ruphis doesn't notice. He's too busy looking at Howard.

Howard looks down at the table. He lifts his eyes to see, no, not Ruphis's eyes, because by now Ruphis is no longer looking at Howard. Herbert is.

But Howard does not see Herbert's eyes, either, even though Herbert is looking right at Howard, and Howard at Herbert. This is because Herbert is wearing sunglasses.

Why is Herbert wearing sunglasses? No one is really sure. Maybe he went to the eye doctor earlier and had his pupils dilated, so his eyes are still incredibly sensitive to light now, even though the interior of the cabin is shrouded in darkness.

Perhaps Herbert simply does not want Ruphis and Howard to see his eyes. He is hiding something, they cannot find it.

Maybe he is trying to look cool, although this is highly doubtful. It doesn't matter, because the eyes are hidden, whatever the reason.

However, Ruphis can now see them. This is because he is seated beside Herbert and can see into the slit between Herbert's glasses and Herbert's eyes.

Then, to Ruphis's dismay, Howard walks across the room, opens up a drawer, and puts on his own pair of sunglasses, without even offering Ruphis a pair.

Why did Howard do that? Is it because he went to the eye doctor earlier and had his pupils dilated, so his eyes are still incredibly sensitive to light, even though the interior of the cabin is shrouded in darkness? Is it because Howard does not want Ruphis and Herbert to see his eyes? If this is the case, what is he hiding? Is he trying to look cool?

Now Ruphis is the only man alive with naked eyes.

Howard returns to the table and is seated.

Ruphis looks at Howard, then nervously shifts his gaze down at his hands on the table.

We're not too sure what Herbert and Howard are looking at, as we cannot see Herbert's and Howard's respective eyes. Howard may be looking at Herbert, or Howard may be looking at Ruphis, or Howard may be looking at both Herbert and Ruphis. Then again, Howard may not be looking at either one of them.

Herbert is probably (I say "probably" even though there is absolutely no evidence in sight to either prove or disprove this potentially fallacious claim) looking at Howard, since Ruphis is seated next to him (Herbert), and yet his head is not tilted in his friend's direction but is at a ninety-five-degree angle with his left shoulder, relatively straight ahead, at the space that is interrupted by Howard's visage.

Then again, it is equally possible that Herbert, keeping his head angled straight ahead at a ninety-five-degree angle (for his head has always tilted a little bit), is straining his eyes to the right of him in a painful attempt to look at his friend Ruphis, although this is highly doubtful, for why wouldn't he just turn his head unless he felt the need to disguise his regard for some dirty secretive reason?

Ruphis is not sure anymore if he's being stared at, for he can no longer see Herbert's eyes as Herbert shifted in his chair a moment ago.

Now it's all a total mystery.

The one thing we may be certain of is that Herbert is not looking at both Howard and Ruphis, as it is physically impossible to do so from Herbert's obtuse positioning in his chair, a bit slumped over, but only figuratively, not literally.

Then again, it is quite possible that Herbert is shifting his gaze back and forth, from Howard to Ruphis, Ruphis to Howard, looking at each for a small amount of time, we'll say 5 seconds each, moving his head and nothing else, Ruphis, Howard, Ruphis, Howard, and so on and so forth ad infinitum.

What if Herbert is not only looking at Ruphis and Howard, but down at the table as well? It's not out of the question, no, yet it is highly doubtful that he looks at the table for the same amount of time he devotes to regarding each of his friends.

Let us thus modify our previous calculation to include the table in our speculations of Herbert's regards. The new chart might look something like this:

Thing Looked At	Time
Howard	51 seconds
Table	30 seconds
Ruphis	40 seconds

since the table is probably the least interesting thing to look at, as it always stays the same, it being made of wood, wood being a solid.

Ruphis breaks the silence to ask Herbert what he's looking at.

Nothing, Herbert replies.

The veracity of Herbert's statement is certainly questionable, although it cannot be simply ignored. For it is possible that the lenses are painted black, restraining Herbert's ability to see anything but blackness.

If this is the case, then is Herbert's statement true or false? May we actually equate blackness with nothing? The answer is Yes and No, spoken aloud simultaneously. The truth is in the lie.

For those seeking a purely positive response to this puzzle, it is not altogether impossible to propose one. For Herbert may have gone blind suddenly, is wearing sunglasses which may or may not be painted black, to shield his eyes, and does not wish to inform Howard and Ruphis of his blindness.

Of course, it is equally possible that one or both of the men are aware of Herbert's hypothetical condition, if it may be called that. It might be best to call it something else, something less specific, but we won't bother doing so.

Suddenly, and for no apparent reason, Howard removes his shades, sliding them over his head where he allows them to rest, tentatively.

What is Howard's motivation for doing this? Are the lenses of the glasses painted black? If so, is Howard troubled by the sight of the blackness of nothingness, or the nothingness of blackness, or the non-sight of the nothingness of blackness, or the non-sight of the blackness of nothingness, or the sight of the non-blackness of nothingness, or the sight of the non-nothingness of blackness, or the non-sight of the non-blackness of nothingness, or the non-sight of the non-nothingness of blackness, or the non-sight of the non-blackness of non-nothingness, or the non-sight of the non-nothingness of non-blackness, or the sight of the non-blackness of non-nothingness, or the sight of the non-nothingness of non-blackness, or the sight of the blackness of non-nothingness, or the sight of the nothingness of non-blackness, or the non-sight of the blackness of non-nothingness, or the non-sight of the nothingness of non-blackness?

Howard has not gone blind, as it has been confirmed that, following the removal of Howard's sunglasses, the following looks were exchanged:

Howard at Ruphis, Ruphis at Howard, Howard at Herbert, Ruphis at the table, Ruphis at Howard, Howard at Ruphis, Ruphis past Howard's head, Ruphis down at his own hands resting on the table, Howard down at Ruphis's hands resting on the table, then over to his own hands resting on his lap, then up at the clock on the wall above Herbert's head, conveniently falling down to Herbert's person, which is still donned in shades.

Meanwhile, Herbert looks at ?, ?, ?, ?, ?, ?, ?, ?, and ?

It occurs to Ruphis that perhaps there is a serious problem with Herbert's eyes. Ruphis considers asking Herbert, then dismisses the thought, because asking a question requires more energy than Ruphis is willing to sacrifice at the present moment.

Howard yawns, letting his glance fall first on Herbert, then, feeling self-conscious in his inability to come to any sort of conclusion on Herbert's hypothetical condition, allows his glance to fall in the ocean of empty space located between where Ruphis and Herbert respectively sit.

This gesture incites Ruphis to glance over at Howard.

Howard holds his lost gaze for a period of approximately 10.6 minutes while Ruphis holds his eyes on Howard for the duration of the time (except for two brief intercessions, the first lasting approximately 15 seconds with the latter lasting a mind-boggling 37 seconds, the first of which is devoted to contemplating a brown stain embodying an area of roughly 3.54490733306245961733324143133818 cubic millimeters resting dormant and hardened approximately 15 centimeters away from where Ruphis's dormant and hardened hands lay resting on the table. Although it may seem absurdly insignificant when compared with the area of the tabletop, $36\pi^2$, the stain seems quite perplexing at the moment in light of all the boring air being passed back and forth between Ruphis and Howard and Herbert [who may actually be a corpse], Howard and Ruphis and Herbert?, Herbert? and Howard and

Ruphis, Herbert? and Ruphis and Howard, Howard and Herbert? and Ruphis, Howard pondering the predicament he now finds himself in while Ruphis ponders Howard's pondering of the predicament he now finds himself in, and thus the stain warrants Ruphis's attention, for he speculates it is a coffee stain, while the second 37-second distraction entails intensely focusing his eyes on another green stain, this one on Herbert's head, which may or may not be mold).

So caught up are they, Ruphis, Howard, Herbert?, in all this watching, they don't even notice when the Men In White enter the cabin, one by one by one, until they are three.

Who are these men and what are they doing in Howard's modest dwelling?

Are they lawyers?

Are they criminals?

Are they policemen?

Are they firemen?

Are they paramedics?

Are they doctors?

Are they thieves?

Are they solicitors?

Are they prostitutes?

Are they priests?

Are they reporters?

Are they enemies?

Are they friends?

Are they family?

Are they brothers?

Are they fathers?

Are they stepbrothers?

Are they stepfathers?

Are they half brothers?

Are they half fathers?

Are they cousins?

Are they uncles?
Are they nephews?
Are they butlers?
Are they lovers?
Are they detectives?
Are they artists?
Are they documentarians?
Are they ministers?
Are they rabbis?
Are they slaves?
Are they servants?
Are they clerks?
Are they libertarians?
Are they anarchists?
Are they Democrats?
Are they Republicans?
Are they Overcomers?
Are they librarians?
Are they graphic designers?
Are they teachers?
Are they interpreters?
Are they prophets, divine interlocutors, Biblical figures?
Are they mechanics?
Are they toy manufacturers?
Are they Internet technicians?
Are they actors?
Are they writers?
Are they signifiers?
Are they frog handlers?
Are they waiters?
Are they bartenders?
Are they builders, construction workers?
Are they scientists?
Are they dog breeders?
Are they juice manufacturers?

Are they nuclear physicists?
Are they brain surgeons?
Are they theoreticians?
Are they religious nuts?
Are they retards?
Are they young?
Are they old?
Are they veterinarians?
Are they judges?
Are they arbitrators?
Are they farmers?
Are they foreigners?
Are they bums?
Are they fast-food employees?
Are they administrative consultants?
Are they administrative assistants?
Are they financial consultants?
Are they small-business owners?
Are they pimps?
Are they receptionists?
Are they fake-vomit manufacturers?
Are they janitors?
Are they dog walkers?
Are they left-handed?
Are they right-handed?
Are they musicians?
Are they engineers?
Are they artisans?
Are they mathematicians?
Are they entertainment producers?
Are they party hosts?
Are they dishwashers?
Are they toilet scrubbers?
Are they hotel managers?
Are they landlords?

Are they flight attendants?
Are they philosophers?
Are they vagrant travelers?
Are they car salesmen?
Are they inventors?
Are they blacksmiths?
Are they geographers?
Are they ichthyologists?
Are they entrepreneurs?
Are they repairmen?
Are they linguists?
Are they speech therapists?
Are they glass-eye salesmen?
Are they oxymorons?
Are they felons?
Are they pipecleaners?
Are they fur dealers?
Are they rhetoricians?
Are they patrons?
Are they nurses?
Are they politicians?
Are they fugitives?
Are they garbage men?
The answer to all of the above questions is no.
For they are too impervious to be lawyers.
Yet they are too saturated in the systematic equation of quotidian existence to be criminals.
They obviously aren't expeditious enough to be policemen.
They are too indelible to be firemen.
They are not frumpy enough to be paramedics.
Nor can it be said that either three are doctors.
And yet they are not thieves. Nor solicitors.
They are too half-hearted to be prostitutes, while not having the disadvantage of being too strict for the brother-hood.

In their mathematical calculations, they lack the heed they need to become efficacious reporters.

They are much too resigned to consider each other enemies, while lacking the pungency that friendship requires.

They also lack the surrogate abstraction familial relations inexorably enjoin: They are not supple enough to be brothers. They feel not the penitence of fathers. They are not self-restrictive enough to be stepbrothers. They are not incestuous enough to be stepfathers. They are not phlegmatic enough to be half brothers. They are not vociferous enough to be half fathers. They are certainly not bucking enough to be cousins. They are scandalously not uncles. They can hardly be called nephews.

They are not ardent enough to be butlers.

They are not slipshod enough to be lovers.

They are too slothful to be detectives.

Fortunately, they are not so flummoxed as to be artists.

Nor can they snoop enough to be called documentarians.

They are not ministers of any denomination I'm aware of.

There's no way in hell they can be rabbis.

They cannot have been slaves, for they are too accessible.

They are not paid enough to be deemed servants.

They are not solvent enough to be clerks.

They are not badgering enough to be libertarians.

They are too badgering to be anarchists.

They are not squally enough to be Democrats.

They are too rank to be Republicans.

They are not ogilarchic enough to belong to the Overcomers.

They are not pale enough to be librarians.

They are not officious enough to be graphic designers.

They are too callow to be teachers.

They are too baffling to be interpreters.

Nary a one of them a prophet, divine interlocutor, or Biblical figure.

They are not robotic enough to be mechanics.

We do not know whether or not they are toy manufacturers, but we can assume that none of them are.

But they are certainly not Internet technicians.

They are not forensic enough to be actors.

They are not scatological enough to be writers.

They are not ambiguous enough to be signifiers.

They are not lubricious enough to be frog handlers.

They are not tall enough to be waiters.

They are not vulnerable enough to be bartenders.

They aren't emotionally stable enough to be builders or construction workers.

They are not sexy enough to be scientists.

Since one of them is half-Asian, none of them can be dog breeders.

They are not naked enough to be juice manufacturers.

They are not neurotic enough to be nuclear physicists.

They are not psychotic enough to be brain surgeons.

They are not soporific enough to be theoreticians.

They are certainly not doughty enough to be religious nuts.

They are not well-endowed enough to be retards.

They are too well-endowed to be either young or old.

None of them can be veterinarians, because two of them have never studied Latin.

They are not monocratic enough to be judges.

They are too judgmental to be arbitrators.

They are too loud to be farmers.

They are too soft to be foreigners.

They are too furry to be bums.

They are too slow to be fast-food employees.

They speak too fast to be administrative consultants.

They speak too slow to be administrative assistants.

They are too fat to be financial consultants.

They are too thin to be small-business owners.

They are too yellow to be pimps.

Victims

They are too black to be receptionists.

They are too brown to be fake-vomit manufacturers.

They are too orange to be janitors.

They are too purple to be dog walkers.

They are too crooked to be left-handed.

They are too straight to be right-handed.

They are too left to be musicians.

They are too right to be engineers.

They are not cosmopolitan enough to be artisans.

How can they be mathematicians when they cannot count?

How can they be entertainment producers when they cannot read?

How can they be party hosts when they are so dull?

How can they be dishwashers when they are so amusing?

How can they be toilet scrubbers when they are so clever?

They cannot be hotel managers because they have no teeth.

They cannot be landlords because they have no eyelashes.

They cannot be flight attendants because they have no mouths.

They cannot be philosophers because they have no cerebellums.

They cannot be vagrant travelers because they have no itinerary.

They cannot be car salesmen. They just can't.

Nor inventors.

Certainly not blacksmiths.

They can't be geographers, they each have a cartographic disorder which prevents such endeavors.

They are too righteous to be ichthyologists.

They are too lethargic to be entrepreneurs.

They are too paltry to be repairmen.

They are too authentic to be linguists.

They are too chatty to be speech therapists.

They are too sophomoric to be glass-eye salesmen.

They aren't artless enough to be oxymorons.
They are too hairless to be felons.
They are too hollow to be pipecleaners.
They are too windless to be fur dealers.
They aren't patronizing enough to be rhetoricians.
They are too rhetorical to be patrons.
They are too obscure to be nurses.
They are too self-fulfilling to be politicians.
They aren't captivating enough to be fugitives.
They are too obsequious to be garbage men.
They are simply the Men In White.

It is thus that the Men In White, although they are not, amongst other things, builders, commence building a white wall in the south end of Howard's cabin.

They use a plaster composed largely of freeze-dried mercury combined with a common metal of unknown origin, forming amalgamic alloys. Thus, the plaster hardens immediately after its removal from the air-tight container and subsequent application.

Of course, the mercury is toxic before it solidifies, so the Men In White are careful to wear white gloves and masks to protect themselves, which conveniently conceals their identity as well, an unnecessary precaution, as Howard is too preoccupied in his starings to notice the fact of their entry, as is Ruphis.

Does Herbert see the Men In White? Or has he become one with the blackness of nothingness, the nothingness of blackness, etc.? There is no way of knowing. Perhaps it would be best to ignore Herbert altogether.

And thus, after their brief performance climaxing in the 10 ft. x 20 ft. wall, the course of its erection clocking in at around 5.163241 minutes, the Men In White disappear, leaving behind Ruphis, Herbert (who, at some point toward the end of the preceding paragraph, suddenly and miraculously removed his shades, revealing what we may only assume is a confirmation of the falsity of the previous death/blind scare chez his person), and Howard, Ruphis staring at Herbert who is focusing his eyes on the blur in front of him that is partly composed of Howard's head, the unseen eyes of which unknown staring back at him (through the shades).

As his eyes adjust to the light or perhaps the lack of light, but surely there must be more light if he was just wearing sunglasses, yet we do not know if he could even see or if the lenses were painted black, so nevermind. We can only make assumptions.

Herbert's eyes focus on Howard, Howard looks back while Ruphis stares at the side of Herbert's head, which suddenly incites Ruphis to look down at his hands now resting side by side in front of him on the table, only 15 centimeters apart, while Herbert looks at Howard, Howard at Ruphis, Ruphis at Howard, Howard at Herbert, Herbert at Ruphis, Ruphis at Herbert, Herbert at Ruphis, Ruphis at the table, Howard at the table, Herbert at Howard, Howard at both Ruphis and Herbert, Herbert at Ruphis, Ruphis at both Howard and Herbert, Herbert at Howard, Howard at Herbert, Herbert at Ruphis, Ruphis at both Herbert and Howard, Herbert at both Howard and Ruphis, Howard and Ruphis exchanging glances, Ruphis and Herbert exchanging glances, Herbert and Howard exchanging glances, Ruphis at Herbert, Herbert at the table, Howard at the table, Ruphis at the table.

Howard sees a wall.

Herbert falls out of his chair.

THE INFORMATION

To the news media

BUICK COUNTY

By the time you read this, we will be gone, several dozen of us. We have completed our task on Earth and have shed our human shells to return to the Next Level of Existence in outer space, from whence we came. This Next Level we speak of is similar to what has been called Heaven or Eternity in sacred literature.

Our task was to offer humanity an entrance into the Next Level of Existence at the end of this millennium, this age, this civilization. Upon entering Earth, we had to enter human vehicles. Now that our task is complete, we have "destroyed" our vehicles through fire, the process required for gaining entry into the Kingdom of Eternity, rebirth into the world of the spirit.

In attempting to educate the world about the Next Level, we were also given the chance to experience first-hand what the Humanoid Level of Existence has become. While this experience has been useful for our larger task, we cannot help but feel sorrow for those who have yet to yield to the call of survival in moving beyond the corruption and hatred this planet has fallen into.

The Next Level is a physical place, inhabited by physical, functioning bodies. However, these bodies are merely shells or vehicles—like a suit of clothes. When an individual's vehicle breaks down, they are given another, and "life" continues. One's true identity lies in the mind or soul of that individual. We thus have no need there for our human vehicles, as our souls have been transported.

No one may enter the Kingdom of Eternity by following the mainstream religious doctrines of "living a good life" and dying. The only way you can enter that Kingdom is when a Representative from the Next Level enters the Earth and instructs you how. Dying doesn't lead you anywhere, except into a hole in the ground.

Periodically, the Next Level dispatches an instructor to the Earth to assist those who are willing to commit to Eternity. The first dispatcher was called Jesus Christ, while ours was given the name Martin Jones.

For those who wish to follow us, it will be incredibly difficult. It requires one to not only believe who we are, but to do as we have done. You must shed all of your human traits in preparation. This includes the greatest sacrifice of all and the ultimate demonstration of faith—the disposal of the human body via the sacred flames of Eternity. If you choose to do this, you must call on the name of Your Father and His Son, Martin Jones, to assist you as you enter into the flames. Your call will be heard by the forces of the Next Level, and you will be picked up by a spacecraft and deported to another world.

Only a member of the Next Level of Existence can rescue you from the fate of death you are otherwise bound to incur. But you are required to sever the final chain that binds you to the Humanoid Kingdom on this planet.

We realize this requires a leap of faith for many of you. But our course has been deliberately designed as a test for those who may be confused as to whether or not they wish to remain in this realm.

We suggest that you enter into the quietest space, the closet of your thoughts, and ask with all your might the Highest Source you can find for guidance. Only those who have been Chosen will know that this is right for them and will be given the courage to act.

THE PACKAGE

After I left Howard's, I went back to the cabin. I was surprised to see a package leaning up against the front door. Written across the middle in black marker was

RUPHIS BOVINE
38 CLIFF'S EDGE DRIVE
MONKHOLE, AMERICA

I was a bit alarmed that whoever sent it knew my last name. People can find out anything about you these days with all those computers and technological shit they got out there. I had never received a package before, and I sure as hell wasn't expecting this one.

I unlocked the front door and immediately locked it behind me once I was inside. I tore off the brown tape and shook the contents out of the huge envelope: a video and a cassette. Something to watch and something to hear. Interesting.

I slipped the video into the dual monitor/VCR device I hadn't used since the day I bought it, many years ago, I don't even remember when. After about a minute of static, a middle-aged woman with a shaved head flashed across the screen. It was cheap, home-video quality recording, with really sterile fluorescent lighting illuminating what looked like a high school cafeteria or something, only totally empty except for this woman, who was clothed in what appeared to be a white bathrobe. Weird.

A man's voice loudly broke the silence almost immediately—I'm assuming he was probably standing right next to the camcorder, filming, perhaps even holding it, it was a bit shaky at first, although it was mostly steady throughout.

. . . Tanya . . . Here . . . Look into the camera, Tanya . . . His voice trailed off.

The woman's head turned to reveal a stunningly plain, androgynous visage, no makeup, the kind of face I might see every day if I saw more people. While it retained a faint trace of youth, patches of weary fatigue and an unnameable darkness of the sort that generally prevails in the faces of much older people bled through the surface, particularly in the area surrounding her eyes, which so violently clashed with the natural rouge of her cheeks. But the eyes themselves, they exuded a cross between open contentment and a deep sadness, revealing more about her life than her words would be able to over the next five-minute span.

. . . uh . . . okay . . .

Hearing her voice led me to recalculate my previous assessment of her eyes; she was on something, you could tell as soon as you heard her. Her lips zombified into a smile as her eyes widened in the camera's glare. She spoke slow, dazed but happy.

Her monologue was initially dotted by several uncertain pauses. She seemed nervous, like she was trying to remember everything she had to say. Her eyes, though, continued speaking an utterly different language. It looked like she had burned out her retinas watching TV on acid or something. The longer she talked, the more she appeared to be taking on the form of something unhuman, something eternal, yet trapped, a prisoner of another dimension.

The smile began to seem almost natural, as the parts of

her that were still able to feel loosened before the camera while she relaxed to the idea of having to express herself. A weary confidence broke through the cracks, climaxing in the ecstatic euphoria of absolute belief.

When she blinked her eyes for the first time and her face twitched, some internal stimuli shifted into gear, perhaps a constipated adrenaline gland finally being released. Then she focused dead-on.

At one point, she lifted up the sleeve of her left arm to reveal a brown bar that had been burned into her skin directly below the shoulder. Apparently, Herbert had one of these too, although I had never seen it. But watching this made me wish I had, as though I needed to somehow confirm what little I knew.

TANYA

I am making this statement as a student about to leave this planet to enter into the Next Level. My objective here is to reflect on my feelings about leaving the world behind. I am making this statement of my own free will.

I first came into contact with My Teacher at a meeting in the desert. As I listened to him speak, it was as though I was already being transported to another level of reality. It was the most extraordinary thing that has ever happened to me. A question or a doubt would pop up in my mind, and then My Teacher would say something like, *Some of you may wonder about . . .* and then state my concern. It was like no one else was in the auditorium, just me in a tunnel with My Teacher on the other side, speaking directly to me, reading my thoughts out loud.

I didn't go into the classroom immediately. A couple months later, I was thinking about the things He had said at that meeting. I remembered him saying, *If you're seeking the purity of Truth, go into the closet of your thoughts and ask with all your might the Highest Source you can channel.* When I did this, I was brought back to that meeting, to that information, and I knew it was high time to enter the classroom of overcoming, to prepare for the Next Level.

I never doubted My Teacher's authority as a Representative of the Next Level. I knew from the start that I had a lot of work to do in overcoming my humanness. At the time, I was very young and pregnant, but My Teacher and fellow students never once judged me or made negative comments about my condition like everyone else in the outside world did—family, friends, doctors. Instead, they were totally positive from the very beginning and never stopped showing support in teaching me how to prepare myself, as well as the shell I was holding inside of me, for the Kingdom of Eternity.

I admit I had some fears in the very beginning. But I knew I had to respond. With Herbert's birth, all of those fears were eliminated. He was immediately accepted as a child of the Next Level, and everyone in the classroom raised him together. I felt like I had finally been reunited with my long lost family.

What's more, everything they said made perfect sense. They didn't solicit new members and they were always up front about the two simple things it takes to get into the Next Level: total commitment and total energy. Those who couldn't handle that kind of self-discipline were encouraged to leave.

The Next Level guided us through an extensive series of individual tests in order to prepare us. One of the most difficult tests I had to endure was several years ago, when Herbert, the human vehicle I gave birth to, left our classroom. At the time, he was the same age I was when I entered the classroom. My human emotions were being tested, and my Family helped me overcome them and move forward. Today, I am a fully evolved being approaching the state of android. I am no longer controlled by my emotions, as I answer to a higher source—the highest source there is, in fact.

I know for a fact that wherever Herbert—that poor lost soul—is, he is not prepared to enter the dimension I am about to enter, for he is tied down, a victim of humanoid distractions that bind him to this lowly planet.

Speaking from experience, when I was out there in the world, I learned about human love, and how shallow and ultimately meaningless it really is, how it turns to hatred and mistrust and deceit in a minute. All endeavors in the human world are, at best, self-serving, self-indulgent, shallow victories, and almost always come at the expense of someone else's pain and misery.

The leaders of this country, of all countries, are hypocritical liars, deceitful scam artists that have no comprehension of Truth whatsoever. Today's governments are beyond corruption—if you look at them closely, you will see that they're no different from Genghis Khan or Hitler. Laws are passed in the name of "keeping the peace," which do nothing but destroy freedom. Wars are fought as a means of "enforcing peace." The contradictions are so rife and self-evident, any sane mind can't help but wonder where the self-appointed gods in positions of power get their authority.

"Success" in the human world is rude, mean, aggressive, abrasive, and distasteful. Why would I want to live in a world that operates under this mentality, that values these features over everything else? You know, based on my experiences in this world, I cannot help but despise it and renounce my citizenship in it.

The only true happiness I've ever known is being with My Teacher, Martin Jones. I know now that I was guided to Him by forces operating above, in the Next Level. I have worked hard with the other students at totally overcoming this world and freeing myself of the traps and addictions you see functioning on every level of society—from the media to institutionalized religion to careers, houses, and families. It's all a trap, it all leads to death. My classmates are the only ones on this planet who truly understand me, who I am and what I've been through, just as I understand who they are and what they've been through.

What my experiences in this classroom have taught me is

that overcoming this world is an individual task—you simply cannot rely on your biological family or friends. Living in the world has taught us that truly meaningful relationships with others are not possible on this planet. Humans were simply not designed to be able to connect with others.

The only meaningful relationship I've had has been with My Father and My Teacher from the Next Level. I am happier and healthier now than I've ever been before. With the direction the world is going in these days, it seems foolish to wish to remain here and dwell in the muck. The inherent goodness and purity of the Next Level simply exceeds what Earth has to offer.

I'm eager to enter Eternity in a new vehicle. If there are humans who view my act of shedding my current shell as crazy or insane, so be it. I have been offered an opportunity that I cannot refuse, to exist in Eternity with My Father. Without Him, I know I am nothing. I can only pity those who are not wise enough to join us on this mission.

MUSIC & SILENCE

A piano beat out a clunky accompaniment that would have probably sounded better had it been strummed on a guitar:

I would even go so far as to call it soothing, or at least pseudo-soothing. Then a choir of . . . people, men and women, young and old, a surprising cacophony of voices resonating a mixed pitch rendition of . . . ? They sang in free-range unison, the recording was bad, making it sound real far away. Leaving the world behind. What had she meant by it? The melody was so weird.

The song was addressed to "My Father." My Father, I Follow Thee to Eternity. Lots of bad rhymes, like "vexed hell" with "Next Level."

And forever shall I quell
my earthly substance of its shell
time will tell
from whence my soul, its cell [. . .]

and the piano interrupted with an uneventful solo before leading the group through a final chorus, repeated thrice for (unsuccessful) effect. A thud as the tape recorder turns off, then a loud whir as it turns back on. I guess they decided to lose the piano for the next track, a wise choice, an *a capella* number. Three voices, two males and a female, painfully attempting to harmonize, stay on key, and in rhythm, but they managed somehow. More "my father leading us" stuff. Some guy gives a short talk about how no human could have designed the course this classroom has taken. A somewhat normal rendition of "Jesus Wants Me for a Moonbeam" [sic]. But Jesus is an alien or, I recall Herbert mentioning something along those lines in the past, but I only barely understood most of the things Herbert said.

I couldn't stand to listen anymore, so I stopped the cassette and relaxed with the silence, the purest music of all. I can't come to any conclusions on this. Do these people really believe a spaceship is gonna land and pick them up? I guess the more important question is: Will it?

L.D.

What is it like to be dead? To go to that big anus in the sky. Utopia. The incredible gaiety of the idea is backwards, an idyllic nun stuck in a closet of skeletons. Yet the impulse of death had superseded every motivation, every rarity of emotion leaking out.

The long weed shot out of the ground. A fly was stuck to a piece of tape.

Memories of nighttime rides through empty towns. Windows rolled down, summertime, thoughts blurred by hashish headaches and too many cigarettes while alone at a four-way intersection, lights red on every side. The soft buzz of neon beneath the half-volume waves of FM radio—the bored voice on the other side. Stores that sell tires and comfortable beds, the way of the suburbs.

Saying thank you to the clerk at the gas station, who stays silent throughout the entirety of the wallet dance. He's seen it countless times before, he'll see it again when the next stoned late-night drifter comes in for a pack of Winstons or a bottle of Mountain Dew, some pork rinds and transmission fluid.

Speeding through the zigzagged streets of this neighborhood, brick houses with basketball hoops and trees, cats dashing under fake Victorian streetlights, red octagons ignored. Folk singer's voice on the radio begs and croaks.

Pulling into driveway. Don't forget to turn headlights off. Or cigarettes on driver's seat. Mom wouldn't be too happy bout that. Aunt Cancer and Uncle Carbon. Sometimes headlights catch a fox's eye, having wandered in from the forest shielded by fur and the suburban silence that comes along with the dark of the moon. Outside light, left on by the caretakers, above garage door. Dispels a circle that barely touches car; enter it.

Lock the door behind, fumble in the dark for light switch. Illuminates interior of garage, Mom's fancy black car, stacks of newspapers, gray trash bins, cobwebs, concrete smooth with dirt. In through the kitchen, hardwood floors. Past Dad's guitar collection, up the stairs, then, through upper passageway—guest bedroom, Dad's office, central hallway, tiptoeing past Mom and Dad's bedroom where they sleep with the door open, silent snores, dreams bestowing the secret wisdom of mediocrity. Into the bathroom for swift beer piss, locking the door behind for no real reason, maybe brush teeth if not too fucked up. Maybe lie in a tub of hot water for a while. Maybe disappear in bedroom, back down hallway, passing once again the resting corpses, white sheets for soil, time can kiss your ass away.

And the signs. *Mechanic's assistant. Cashier wanted. Jesus Christ is the light of the world.* Vacant storefronts. Restaurant *closed* signs. Neon buzz. Dry breeze.

Laying back, two pillows under your head. Maybe touch yourself beneath the covers. Maybe just stare ahead, into the dark, until you can see golden molecules circling round the sludge of air. Buried. Pendulum of thoughts swinging down closer to your body, cutting the tired wind. Finally granted with the throttle of space, drift off into the airs of change. Soon, all is hue in perspective.

Across town, there is a two-room house in which the TV stays on all night. Man in a chair sits in front of it. Blue jeans, baseball cap, and no shirt in armchair. Drinks his silence.

You say goodbye to this and goodnight to that and walk quietly down the stairs through the kitchen into the room on the side of the house, by the garage, where Dad keeps his guitar collection. You take a set of guitar strings from out of the drawer and tie them around your neck. Oak tree in front yard. That's how you want the morning to find you.

The silver cows carried on a conversation. The stars in the sky were shattered dots. No one was awake to see them. Center of sharing beneath the skin. Two brains beat back and forth. Evil is removed from every situation. Glad dogs revel. The future a cold piece of toast. Glad fathers the furtive gestures. Fat wheels on each side of a long stick. Sad woman long hair sits with sunglasses on. Foot explosion. Grocery store grumbles. Line zit on the side of yellow. I yr drown you. Motivate mother to pick up the knife wound. The big long thing stretches. I think it is called a cat in most places. Nipple the bunter on to grandiose. The shovel realizes how to be flat. Zoological barks a name. Shadows, the best kind of gesture. Smoke being spat out knows what toenail is created. Down in the factory, I always knew my name. How am I allowed to see you, prudence? You can't even spell backwards. Sunglass avenue no me clean . . . Something squirts out of the deformed bird up above. Novel beginnings, the cheese of a lie. The ground is a chaos of symbols.

VICTIMOLOGY

The day stumbles upon Ruphis stumbling into the International House of Pancakes in the county of Buick, where he immediately places an order for coffee and a Rooty Tooty Fresh 'N Fruity breakfast. Ruphis informs the young waitress that he likes his eggs scrambled well and his meat cooked crisp. His plate arrives one minute later. Lifting his fork in advance of a forthcoming display of fantastic implication, this bold and adventurous meal-seeker proceeds to cut up all the contents of his Rooty Tooty Fresh 'N Fruity and blend them together—scrambled eggs, bacon, sausage, pancakes, and all—finishing off the whole fantastic orgy with a few climactic not to mention impervious squirts of blueberry syrup for the sake of both consistency and symmetry, stirring it all together like a painter might be found alone late at night in his studio mixing paints for an unending canvas, going nowhere. Of course, this is not true because the art, in this case, was indeed going somewhere, that somewhere being Ruphis's stomach, followed by the toilet.

In the right pocket of Ruphis's blue jeans, a smooshed piece of paper with a blurry address scrawled in blue ballpoint pen, not a street, an avenue, nor a boulevard, but a "route," Route 7, to be precise, 3247 Route 7 in the county of Buick, Buick Elementary School, to be even more precise.

Victims

A couple of fat women sit behind him—one black, one white—donned in Sunday dress, discoursing quietly on the news. He doesn't eavesdrop on their conversation. No, Ruphis is preoccupied with mixed sentiments regarding his inopportune positioning in the trials and tribulations of the day. For he didn't come here, to this town, to eat breakfast. He came to find some answers.

Howard, melting into the slabs of wood making up the floor of his cabin, attempting to bust through, so to speak, the white wall, but not succeeding. Insane with curiosity, what-ever it is waiting for him on the other side. He can hear it breathing while he lies in bed, trying to will himself into sleep. Occasionally, the thing emits a wild yelp, as though it's getting killed or fucked by some mysterious force. He can't sleep. Yet even blinder at night than during the day. Wall growing thicker and thicker as each hour passes.

One afternoon, he looks in the mirror to see an empty, naked shell where once he had seen himself, or at least the body he had taken for granted as a self. *Maybe*, he thought, *it is a case of mistaken perception. As though some foreign faculty of my imagination has suddenly reared its head so late in life, materializing as a symbol that appears to be as real as it actually isn't. But if this is so, it has already deceived each of my senses in the passage of time, so it's highly un-likely that my mind alone is responsible for its mysterious presence.*

Still, the idea of having somehow willed it into existence remains a passive option in the days that follow, background noise to return to after every other hypothesis fails. The wall's force is felt more and more as the days drag on. Howard beats his fists against it and wonders if it is really as hollow as it seems. As a child, he had read a story about people who lived in walls, and he remembered how bad it had frightened him, how he was convinced for years afterwards that these wall people surrounded him when he was alone, unseen. The harder he hits, the more hopeless it seems, until he gives up trying to conquer it through violence and enters the contemplative phase of his relationship with what he now regards as a blank object.

Ruphis feels like he is trapped in a blue nightmare with all the coffee he could possibly want to drink, the smiling waitresses killers in disguise, the fat scum redneck invalids supposed to blend in with the grease landscape, instead somehow involved in the conspiracy, stringy stares and all. Despite, or perhaps due to his apprehensions about this weighty thing in his pocket, this flaccid scrap of paper, Ruphis sits there, paralyzed. I will stay here and watch him.

Look at the blue screen in front of you. Look at the sky. There is no one else out there. But look at the lights that hover above, in the clouds. Humpty Dumpty cracked his skull open on the hardwood floor. Perhaps this study is inconclusive. The time comes to bang one's head. Various household objects are used as props in what is ultimately a play, a theatrical performance—a frying pan, a hammer, anything heavy and terse enough to . . . not necessarily chip away frustration. Let us avoid facile psychological explanations. Instead of running away at an opportune moment, the victim will always stay. Those silly victims! Those haha abstracts of reality! Their brains whacked like pecan pie: Whack! in the head. One more time. May have actually succeeded in stunning myself. Perhaps a little faster. Ding! (The pan echoes. Echo is prolonged in the assertive one's brain. Was this experiment yielding "positive" results? [Were the lights in the victims' eyes more luminous than ever before?])

Herbert kept falling down. One day, Ruphis divulged the contents of the package. In yet another rare display of emotion, Herbert's eyes widened with fear as a growing panic overtook him. That threat of eternity he thought he had escaped suddenly bit him in the nose.

The next day, he disappeared.

Ruphis was unable to find him for days, until one cloudy afternoon he was walking down the street when he passed by a ditch and heard a loud, guttural groan. Ruphis walked over to find his friend curled up in a blanket.

What are you doing down there?

I'm scared.

They didn't say anything else to each other, but Ruphis understood his unspoken fear, the possibility that They would find him—no matter how well he hid himself, he wasn't invisible to that kind of force. He didn't want to go with Them. So he disappeared the only way he knew how.

The day Herbert's Final Fall (as it would come to be known) took place, he had begun drinking his whiskey at dawn. He read the Bible and shook a tambourine. He walked outside and watched as the last stars died away.

Undoubtedly, questions will pop up from each moral post. Although every possible crime may be committed, it is important to note that the most fascinating ones are the ones we commit against ourselves, both intentional and in spastic waves of careless error. For example: If something is in your way, why not break it with your head?

I've never asked for forgiveness. But I've said many a prayer. I walked down to the train. From up in my house on the hill, I could hear its whistle blowing. I took my vows, devoted myself to the tree. The simple joys of living—it got to be they overwhelmed me. I couldn't stand it. I couldn't be that. Didn't have to be. The pain of last September. Or a parade of immobile spectres, one-eyed cows versus the veterans of every conceivable war. Some can't cry. Others can't feel. Some can only feel pain. Others can only experience joy. Artificial alive. Water and bread.

They stand in a circle of silence, staring ahead with bright smiles slashing through their faces, sparks in the holes of their eyeballs, anticipating their rebirth into the new. Some had taken pills, Ketamine, to ease the inevitable pains of the shedding process, but the majority feel only the substance-less together, a unanimous rush through the bodies they are about to lay down.

The hoods on their heads poking up toward the sky, like horns. Martin stands in the center, a flaming torch above his head pointed at the skies, signaling His Father.

One by one, each hood blessed with the sacred fire, born of spirit, until He stands in the center, a ring of fire, human candles, and screams, ecstasy not pain, the odor of flesh melting off bones like wax.

Closing his eyes, He lets the flame drop onto his own hood, following his disciples, leaving this place behind for the second time.

He slides the greasy plate next to a near-empty cup of coffee. A dirty napkin, a blue mini-gunrack of flavored syrup containers, salt and pepper, a fake-marble holder of sugars and fake sugars, a shot glass filled with cream.

I walked to the sink to get him a glass of water. He stunk, naked and yellow. I assumed he was no longer writing, because his typewriter had been pissed and shat in. It smelled rancid, like death. He was sitting there pathetically on the floor with a big bruise on his forehead. The table had been overturned. He slapped the glass out of my hand. Thankfully, I caught it before it hit the floor, spilling water all over myself. Then he took the empty glass out of my hands and smashed it into his forehead, hitting the ground in a collision of blood and glass.

Are you okay?

In response to my panicked inquiry, he rose, with a piece of glass sticking out of his forehead, and proceeded to run straight ahead into the wall that now formed a side of his quadrangle dwelling. You could hear his bones smacking as he hit against it and was then thrown back down against the floor. For some reason, it reminded me of a ping pong ball shooting out of a cave.

I stood over him looking down at the cluttered mess he'd become. He opened his eyes and stared up at me, blinking fast, dazed.

I can't know, he said. *I can't know.*

When the waitress walks past his table, Ruphis stops her with a gesture and orders a glass of orange juice.

As the flames grow out of His vehicle, He sees the bright yellow flames of the spacecraft descending before Him. He screams joyfully as he feels not the needle-like pain of burning flesh ridding itself of his vehicle, but the everlasting sensation, the one true sensation there is, of righteousness burning through his soul.

A ramp is lowered, and the androids, who look remarkably human-like despite their advanced features—wider eye sockets, remnants of ears and nose, smooth, rubbery skin—descend with tools in hand to sift through the burnt offerings, searching for the requirements of their task. One by one, they pry out the minds from each of the thirty-nine bodies, leaving behind what remains of the human shells they had been trapped in.

Beneath the circular craft, a gaping hole, a void, or so it seems, emits an odorless smoke. The androids transport the minds to this hole, whereupon they insert them, one at a time, as the engine begins to sing: a hollow buzz, more like a mechanical vibration.

Reboarding the craft, the androids resume their posts at their work stations. Having finally found the fuel they required, they can continue their journey back to the universe from whence they came.

The hours find Ruphis still stuck to the blue leather seat at IHOP, absently staring out the window at the parking lot, drifters and sinners from Buick, Monkhole, the next town over, the one after that, etcetera, and so on, come and go, and yet he sits and wonders and watches them all. He goes so far as to ask the waitress if she could point him toward this Buick Elementary School, pointing to the blue address scrawled in the torn palm-sized paper.

But there hasn't been a Buick Elementary School in years!

Victims

Where am I? Where has the time gone? What year? How long ago? Who are my friends? What did I go looking for? Why?

Travis Jepperson

The isthmus of the apocalypse reared its ugly head in the direction of the North Star, challenging any and all opposing allegories to get into shape before the year exhaled her last breath, leaving a thousand housewives to tear up coupons in back alleys of dim sums.

Blue lights flamed out of the dark nowhere, creating a spare entrance into the void it seems no one cared about. Springs jerked and sprung, left and right, creating a certain cathartic disorder that left paralyzed the unhinged want in Martin's knee. Sprawling flowers like welcoming signs of the devil shitted venomously into the no-good third realm, every division asphyxiating itself onto him like some sort of perilous rapture, earth colliding with wind. Bred sorrows from layered minds. Squabbles directionless like the tire caused from a sprout of lightning. Shit tones in the air. Abandoned fires— the silence off of every ear. Then, the next ray of blessing, stale cigarette smoke to clothing. Blood the maggot of wildfire, jestering at ruletime palace. Elastic yellow kids wishing to give it up. Tools of time, tool of every place. This, uninhabited by most spheres of justice, this, syntopic humanoid.

Also from AKASHIC BOOKS

HIGH LIFE by Matthew Stokoe

326 pages, a trade paperback original, $16.95, ISBN: 1-888451-32-7

A selection of the **Little House on the Bowery** series

"Stokoe's in-your-face prose and raw, unnerving scenes give way to a skillfully plotted tale that will keep readers glued to the page . . . Stokoe's protagonist is as gritty and brutal as they come, which will frighten away the chaste crowd, but the author's target Bret Easton Ellis audience could turn this one into a word-of-mouth success."

–Publishers Weekly

THE ICE-CREAM HEADACHE by James Jones

235 pages, trade paperback, $13.95, ISBN: 1-888451-35-1

"The thirteen stories are anything but dated . . . a compact social history of what it was like for Mr. Jones's generation to grow up, go to war, marry, and generally, to become people in America."

–The Nation

SEED by Mustafa Mutabaruka

*Selected for the *Washington Post's* Best Novels of 2002 list*

*Selected for *Library Journal's* Best First Novels of Spring/Summer 2002 list*

178 pages, trade paperback, $14.95, ISBN: 1-888451-31-9

"Mutabaruka's deft maneuvering between past and present, Morocco and the United States, blurs distinctions and creates a mystical and frightening story . . . [P]lain prose and interesting characters keep this novel on its feet and make it dance."

–Library Journal

SUICIDE CASANOVA by Arthur Nersesian

370 pages, hardcover binding into hard-plastic videocassette,

$25.00, ISBN: 1-888451-30-0

"Sick, depraved, and heartbreaking–in other words, a great read, a great book. *Suicide Casanova* is erotic noir and Nersesian's hardboiled prose comes at you like a jailhouse confession."

–Jonathan Ames, author of The Extra Man

ADIOS MUCHACHOS by Daniel Chavarría

Winner of a 2001 Edgar Award

245 pages, paperback, $13.95, ISBN: 1-888451-16-5

"Daniel Chavarría has long been recognized as one of Latin America's finest writers. Now he again proves why with *Adios Muchachos*, a comic mystery peopled by a delightfully mad band of miscreants, all of them led by a woman you will not soon forget—Alicia, the loveliest bicycle whore in all Havana."

—Edgar Award-winning author William Heffernan

IT'S A FREE COUNTRY: Personal Freedom In America After September 11
Edited by Danny Goldberg, Victor Goldberg, and Robert Greenwald

Contributors include Cornel West, Michael Moore, five members of the US Congress, Howard Zinn, Ani DiFranco, Matt Groening, Tom Hayden, and many others

370 pages, hardcover, $19.95, ISBN: 0-9719206-0-5

"A terrific collection about civil liberties in our society. We must never forget that we live in our faith and our many beliefs, but we also live under the law—and those legal rights must never be suspended or curtailed." —Reverend Jesse Jackson

SOME OF THE PARTS by T Cooper

Selected for the Barnes & Noble Discover Great New Writers Program

264 pages, trade paperback, $14.95, ISBN: 1-888451-36-8

"Sweet and sad and funny, with more mirrors of recognition than a carnival funhouse, *Some of the Parts* is a wholly original love story for our wholly original age."

—Justin Cronin, author of *Mary and O'Neil*
(2002 PEN/Hemingway Award Winner)

Travis Jeppesen was born in Fort Lauderdale in 1979. His writing has appeared in *Book Forum*, *Low Blue Flame*, *3am Magazine*, *The Stranger*, *The Prague Pill*, and other publications. He is a contributing editor to *Pavement Magazine* and a columnist for the German music website Dorf Disco. *Neomania*, Jeppesen's screenplay based on Lautreamont's *Maldoror*, death metal, and teenage serial killers, is currently in preproduction. Having resided in Charlotte, Seattle, New York, Paris, Amsterdam, and Berlin, Jeppesen currently resides in an undisclosed Eastern European country. *Victims* is his first novel.